UNDER THE EYES OF THE CONDOR

Copyright © 2010 - Dick Roberts and Deeds Publishing
Printed in the United States of America

Cover design by Mark Babcock

Published by Deeds Publishing, Marietta, GA

First Edition, October 2010

For information write Deeds Publishing, PO Box 682212, Marietta, GA 30068 or www.deedspublishing.com

ISBN 978-0-9826180-6-6

UNDER THE EYES OF THE CONDOR

By

Dick Roberts

To Heather

To Roy Hebert

Good reading

Deeds Publishing

www.deedspublishing.com

ACKNOWLEDGEMENT

I wish to thank my wife Roberta for her patience and aid in accomplishing the completion of this tale.

INTRODUCTION

This story began in the Department of Cochabamba, Bolivia, in September 1964. A military coup replaced Víctor Paz Estenssoro, the revolutionary president elected after the National Revolutionary Movement, (Movimiento Nacionalista Revolucionario), Agrarian Reform of 1952. The ranches (fincas) were deserted by the wealthy landowners and taken over by the farmers (campesinos) in an attempt to extract subsistence from the arid soil of the mountain slopes.

The military coup was the result of the ultimate co-operation between Ovando Candia, General of the Armies, and Renee Barientos Ortuno, General of the Bolivian Air Force.

General Overdo Candia was of Spanish ancestry while Renee Barientos Ortuno's father was Spanish and his mother was Quechua. They not only co-operated as leaders of the coup, but continued on as co-presidents.

General Candia was the strong man of the duo and enforced government policies.

General Barientos was the popular charismatic leader well in tune with the rural population of Bolivia. A year and a half later he was drafted by the general population to run for election.

A number of projects were planned and started in the mid 1960's to provide electric power and water for the tin mines in Oruru. A major highway was started between Cochabamba and Santa Cruz.

During these times it was not at all unusual to encounter truck loads of armed campesinos arriving in the urban areas to voice their desire for Barientos to run for election.

He at last bent to the will of the people and won the election with a reported 80% of the vote.

He was instrumental in setting education requirements for all Bolivian children and aiding in the development of oil and gas production in the Santa Cruz area.

As president he invited the U.S. military to help train an elite airborne unit and counter insurgency teams trained by the U.S. Army Special Forces.

The newly trained military were responsible for the capture of Che Guevera (a Cuban revolutionary) while he was trying to develop a communist regime in Bolivia.

Unfortunately Barientos died in a fiery helicopter crash in 1969.

DICK ROBERTS

This is a fictionalized account of happenings in Bolivia in the 1960's. The author, his wife Irene, and their five children lived in Cochabamba from 1964 to 1966.

CHAPTER 1

MONDAY, FEBRUARY 24, 1969

As the jeep moved slowly along a back street, the driver reached his hand down into his left boot and retrieved a .22 caliber pistol. Slamming on the brakes, he brought the jeep to a sudden stop. He took the opportunity of the sudden stop to turn to his right and fire the pistol at the back of his passenger's head. The bullet did not kill his passenger immediately, but left him paralyzed.

"What was that noise? Sounded like a small balloon bursting," the passenger thought.

"That gun he has in his hand. Can't feel anything. Must be shock. Damn it, I didn't frisk the bastard. He had a gun stuck in his boot. Should've known better. Seem to be paralyzed. Can't move my arms or legs. Wonder where he plans to dump my body," he thought as he was fighting unconsciousness. Finally… blackness.

It was another beautiful morning in the Cordirilla Oriental (Eastern Mountain Range of the Andes) in Bolivia. Pedro had passed through the junction in the road from Santa Cruz to Cochabamba and the road to Colomi. He'd made the one-direction trip up from Via Tunari yesterday to the road junction just east of Cochabamba. Pedro Gonzales and his passengers with their truckload of coca leaf had stayed at the chicharria (native rest stop, serving chicha) near the junction. They'd had their fill of chicha (Andean corn beer, most often made from maize) and chicharron (deep fried pork), so they were ready to leave at sun-up for the ride to Cochabamba.

The heavily loaded truck wound its way up the mile long switchback, climbing from 10,000 feet to 12,000 feet at the cumbre (mountain pass). The truck rounded the curve at the crest of the cumbre, just as the sun rose behind Pedro and his passengers, cascading the 16-foot wide road in a blaze of light. Shadows broke over the side of the road obscuring the canyon 500 feet below.

Pedro kept the truck as far to the right as he could, up against the near vertical mountain side above them. It was most fortunate that he did keep to the far right, as a grey Jeep came charging up the grade straight at him. The Jeep veered right, missing the truck by a few inches. Then the Jeep rounded the curve in a cloud of flying pebbles and dust. Pedro could only see particles of dust, billowing in the bright sunlight behind him at the curve. He kept driving toward Cochabamba. That was his job.

It has truly been said that nothing happens in the mountains of Bolivia without a witness. That was true in this case. A giant Andean Condor was gliding high above the crest of the mountain, scouring the landscape for his lunch. His wings were unmoving, the feathers at his wingtips moving slightly to keep him on course. His head, with its six inch beak, moved from side to side, continually searching.

There! Something moved. The condor wheeled right to check out the movement. Something was rolling down the side of the mountain toward the canyon. It was a large object very unlike any morsel of food that he recognized. The condor continued on its search.

A young boy of about six years of age was picking up potatoes with his brother and two sisters. Their mother was digging the potatoes, admonishing them not to throw potatoes at each other. She cuffed one of the boys on the side of the head to get his attention. The younger boy looked away toward the far canyon wall just below the road. He saw a large cloud of dust as something rolled end over end down the canyon wall. He called to his mother. It was much too late for her to see anything, so she told him to stop day dreaming and get back to picking up potatoes.

High up on the side of the mountain, across the canyon from the road, an eight year old girl was tending her flock of sheep. She was always on the lookout for condors that might swoop down to fly off with one of the lambs. She had her single rope sling and a supply of rocks in her bag along with wool that she was continuously spinning into yarn. She was constantly on the lookout when she saw a large cloud of dust and a faint outline of a grey Jeep rolling end over end down the canyon wall.

CHAPTER 2

SAN FRANCISCO, CALIFORNIA, ONE MONTH EARLIER

Fog shrouded The Embarcadero, hiding the Golden Gate Bridge and the San Francisco-Oakland Bay Bridge. The Richmond-San Raphael Bridge was barely visible through the veil of fog. Market Street was somewhere down below the BOSCO (Big Office In the Sky Construction Company) main office, located on the 30th floor of the Bank of America Building on California Street.

Al Provo looked out the window to see the South Tower of the Golden Gate Bridge, peaking up through a blanket of fog. This was the rainy time in San Francisco, when it not only rained but it tended to pour in sheets of water, drowning the streets. Today was the exception to that general occurrence.

Al was recalling the New Year's Eve party at the Lounge in Ghiradeli Square. He had met a long legged brunet beauty that professed to like to party with him. Her dark brown eyes sparkled every time she looked at him. He would have to call her for a return engagement.

He sipped his espresso coffee and decided that it was time to get to work.

"Finally, a clean desk. What a bunch of crap I've piled up this past month."

Al ran his hands over his blond crew cut, left over from his Korean War days.

"Now I can start that review of those design documents for the Hi-Speed Rail Tunnel Project in California which sure did need a lot of PR to get the voters to approve funding."

Al's phone rang several times before he picked it up, "Hello, Provo speaking. Yes, you have the right Albert Provo, Oh! What is this all about? I understand, but why me? Are these orders on the up and up? When am I supposed to arrive there? You said Saturday morning and I will be contacted there?"

Al sat back in his chair and let his mind wander back about three years to his last mission to Bolivia. He thought, "I was able to ferret out the insurgent's leader and he was dealt with in the customary manner. I damned near bought the farm on that one. Well, shit, this one sort of snuck up on me."

About twenty minutes later John Christman called to Al, "Please come to my office. I just had a very strange phone call concerning you. The American State Department has requested that you be in Cochabamba, Bolivia, not later than this coming Saturday morning."

The phone went dead as Al headed for John's office.

"Ok! Just what the hell is this all about, Al? I know you have some kind of connection with the U.S. Government, but why all this cloak and dagger stuff?"

Al shrugged his shoulders to indicate that he did not have the foggiest idea. Actually he thought to himself that he knew that the caller represented the CIA.

John Christman was his leader and CEO in the main office of BOSCO.

"Fortunately this call came at an appropriate time; the project manager on the Trans Andean Tunnel wired me last week asking to have you sent to Bolivia for a few months to help them out."

"So, how would you like to go to Bolivia for a couple of months?" John asked, leaning over his desk. "Your airline tickets will be delivered before noon. I do assume that you can catch the flight out at 5:30 PM for Lima, Peru, Friday January 17th with connections to La Paz and Cochabamba, Bolivia. That's where the caller told me that you were to go."

Coming from John, that was not a request, it was a directive. After all he was the CEO of BOSCO.

Al's mind was racing. He was being made a bit uneasy by John's inquiring stare. Al realized that he needed to play the innocent, so as not to blow his cover, as it were.

"Where the hell is Bolivia?" Al asked. "I know it's not in North America, but I gather it must be somewhere near Peru. Right?"

Al knew John knew nothing about his last trip down there. He might as well play dumb on this area.

"Ah! Mr. Provo! You jest. You'll just love it down there. Senoritas and carnivals and Bolivian drinks, in addition to all those beautiful mountains and exotic scenery. With your ability in Spanish you should have no trouble finding a brown eyed brunet. BOSCO has a hydro tunnel there that's in bad trouble. They've been having major rock falls that have trapped the Tunnel Boring Machine (TBM). The folks on the job have no idea what to do about saving the TBM, or the project. I want you to go down there and straighten that mess out. Take warm clothes; the tunnel's at an altitude of 12,000 feet."

With that bombshell, John waved Al back to his office, leaving Al to search his computer files to find out what he was about to get involved in. Well! So much for the long legged brunet with the dark brown eyes.

Al drove back to his condo to leave a message with the condo manager that he would be "missing" for a few months. The condo was near the top of Lombard Street (claimed as being one of the steepest streets in the world). The view of the San Francisco Bay and all the bridges were unsurpassed. Alcatraz and Angel Island were all part of the landscape. He always felt a twinge of regret when he had to leave for other cities, if even for a short time. He hoped there would be no fog in Bolivia.

CHAPTER 3

Sam, his part time drinking buddy who managed the condos, was used to Al's absences. He always said the same thing to Al: "Don't those people you work for ever give you any notice? I don't know how you manage. Good thing you don't have to juggle a woman and a condo manager."

Remembering how Sam had laughed and laughed to himself last month when Al had taken off so quickly for a week up in Labrador, Al smiled to himself as he wrote a quick note, asking Sam to please forward any mail to the office, and to please leave a few good looking girls for him. Al had no other entanglements, so there was no need to notify anyone else.

Thursday evening he packed his travel and work clothes, including boots and some dress clothes for the hoped-for partying when he had some time off the job.

Al reflected that he had once been a happily married man. He took his airborne training at Fort Benning, Georgia, where he enjoyed working with his platoon in training. He was assigned a platoon in Korea. Because he had shown an aptitude for long range patrols, it was natural for him to volunteer for a mission to free a number of POW's being held by the North Koreans. He accomplished that mission without a scratch. He was awarded a Silver Star and a promotion.

The day he was discharged from the army, his wife was killed in an automobile accident on her way to pick him up. He hit the bottle - and after a month, someone who had known of his exploits in Korea contacted him. During his drying out he agreed to a job with the CIA. Their proposal was almost too good to be true. They would use their influence to place him as a tunnel engineer with BOSCO. In return he would agree to short covert missions as needed. He would be well paid and would be able to travel. What could be more ideal to a recent widower - ideal until his first mission where he had an opportunity to see one of the bad guys carried out in a body bag.

Al Provo seemed to have promoted himself to the position of a corporate trouble shooter by virtue of having several successful projects to his credit. Somebody in the Big Office in the Sky seemed to have it in their mind that Al could walk on water and never even cause a ripple. Oh well! It made for an adventurous life with a very good bank account. Al never complained, primarily as no one would listen with a sympathetic ear if he did.

Friday morning Al woke up to fog, as usual. He thought to himself that at least the limo wouldn't have any problems, since he wasn't leaving until after noontime.

At the San Francisco International Airport he checked in at the South American Airlines counter. The pleasant young lady serving as the ticket agent was extremely helpful and made him feel welcomed. Fortunately his passport and visas were all up to date.

As expected, the plane had a mechanical problem. The usual suspects were birds flying around. The backup on the tarmac was horrendous. Naturally, the plane would be an hour late leaving. Al's only consolation was that the Boeing 727 had reasonably comfortable first class accommodations. The plane was finally airborne, headed for a quick stop at Colon, Panama, then on through to Lima, Peru.

The four hour flight was made more comfortable by the continuous attention of a very trim good looking brunet flight attendant who kept him well supplied with both Scotch and congenial conversation. Too bad she was only going as far as Lima.

It was close to midnight, and the sky was surprisingly clear, when Al stepped from the plane and made his way down the steps. Walking toward the terminal, he rubbed his eyes.

No sleep tonight, he thought. I'll make up for it tomorrow when I get into Bolivia. I'll at least have the week end to catch up. It should be nice and quiet until Monday. Hope there's some kind of message for me at the hotel desk from the guy I'm coordinating with. What's his name? Ah, yes – Bob Adams.

Al quickly read the sign directing him to the underground passages leading to the international ticket desk. He noted the many grim looking para-military types with sub-machine guns. These men made him feel much safer as every one of them glared at him as if he were about to start a revolution. Their ill fitting uniforms didn't have the normal military creases in the trousers. The young soldiers, if that's what they were, seemed to be in a perpetual slouch except for their fingers which were lovingly caressing the triggers of the sub-machine guns.

The check-in was efficient and Al quickly boarded a South American Airlines flight, another Boeing 727 bound for Rio de Janeiro, with an intermediate stop in La Paz, Bolivia. The plane was full of European doctors headed for a big medical conference in Brazil. The pilot was very thoughtful; he banked the plane on its wing tip so everyone could have a very complete and nauseating view of El Misti.

The local volcano, topping out at 19,101 feet, had last erupted in 1784. Al could barely see the volcano around all the upturned butts of the doctors obstructing the view. The obstructions soon moved back to their seats and their barf bags. Al thought that it merely looked like another hole in the ground except for all of the strange volcanic boulders spewed out onto its rim.

The pilot's voice came crackling into the cabin.

"This volcano is but one of the sixteen volcanoes in Peru, all greater than 15,000 feet in elevation. Enjoy a great view."

The view was one of brown mountain slopes completely lacking in trees. Rock outcrops were evident throughout the line of flight. Occasionally small villages were seen at the ends of mountain trails, passable only by llama and burros. Corn and potato patches dotted the landscape as the plane flew over.

This gyration gave those with strong stomachs a clear view of the smoking volcano. The majority of the passengers were too busy with their barf bags.

The new crew consisted of wasp-waisted Latina flight attendants, several of whom had great interest in spoken English. Al was as accommodating as he could possibly be, as they were all charming company. The unfortunate situation was that they were all going through to Rio de Janeiro.

They flew up and over the Western ridge of the Andes with snow capped peaks extending up to well over 20,000 feet. This range provided the border with Peru and Chile. All of these peaks were sharp points of shear knife edged rock pointing toward the sky, the result of cataclysmic uplifts of the rock and soil. The peaks were interrupted by deep canyons dropping to raging rivers below. The pilot reduced cabin pressure from a comfortable 8,000 feet to 13,000 feet altitude to prepare the passengers for the high altitude of LaPaz.

They flew over a portion of Lago Titacaca, the largest and deepest lake in South America. The surface of the lake formed a border between Peru and Bolivia at about 13,000 feet above sea level. This area of the Andes was the site of the Tiwanacuan and Incan empires.

Al again de-planed, only this time it was at the La Paz-El Alto International Airport. The 13,500-foot altitude of the airport quickly made Al learn rather rapidly that one did not want to start jogging or doing any exercise for a while. He could see Mt. Illimani in the distance as its snow-capped glaciated peak topped out at 21,122 feet.

Stopping briefly by a faded travel poster, Al read rapidly in Spanish:

"There are twenty peaks in Bolivia, ranging from 16,000 feet to 21,463 feet above sea level. The Altiplano is above 13,500 feet and runs most of the length of Bolivia. The Altiplano is a vast table land nearly completely devoid of trees. The only vegetation is the sparse grass that seems to cover most of the high country of Bolivia."

Accompanying these solemn words was a bleak, treeless colorless countryside.

CHAPTER 4

"Well, hell. This is not going to be one of my better trouble-shooting forays. Nothing's going to happen here, that's for sure."

The airport terminal was a squat two story concrete block structure that did little to entice one to stick around any longer than he had to. The lower floor housed the baggage and customs/immigration offices while the upper floor was the ticketing area. This area did have large picture windows so that one could see the expanse of mountains surrounding the airport.

Al was herded through customs and immigration by some rather stern looking officials. The military was well represented at every corner. Al, of course, reported to them that he was just visiting Bolivia as a tourist. They stamped his passport and directed him on to his connecting flight to Cochabamba. Al boarded an old Douglas DC-7 sitting on the tarmac. Rumor had it that there had originally been three of the DC-7's. One had apparently tried to bore through one of the mountains in an effort to conserve fuel. The third plane was only allowed to land in Bolivia, as it defied all criteria having to do with its being airworthy. Al and his fellow passengers sat there for about an hour, sucking on oxygen to keep from turning blue. The oxygen, at least, seemed to provide a slight taste to the air, a clean taste.

The plane finally waddled down the 12,000 feet long runway and lifted off, just barely, over the city of La Paz. The four radial Pratt and Whitney engines cried in pain as they were stressed to their limits. The plane did not gain a lot of altitude; instead it dropped about 500 feet as it left the runway. Al was not certain that they would gain enough altitude to fly over the surrounding peaks, rather than through them.

The craggy mountain peaks reared up at them as they headed for Cochabamba. There was no vegetation above 10,000 feet. Most of the brush has long since been cut for fires in the campesinos' adobes. The only trees visible were those springing up in the deep canyons. Those were eucalyptus trees replanted from Australia many years ago. The sterile bright blue lakes slid below them as the sides of the mountains were being passed by their wingtips.

It soon developed into a very bumpy ride from all the updrafts coming up the steep vertical walled canyons. Al was quite relieved when they made their approach to the Cochabamba airport, until they circled the airport. He felt that if the landing gear had been down they would have touched the slopes of Mt. Tunari at 17,000 feet as they passed through roiling thunderheads. The Cochabamba airport sat at about 8,500 feet with one runway ensconced between high mountain peaks.

Al remembered reading that Cochabamba is centered in a basin between two converging mountain ranges. The entire valley is approximately 15 miles from one end to the other.

"A nice long hike on the ground, but a very short space for an airplane dropping some 9,000 feet in the space of 7.5 miles," he thought to himself.

The terminal was a rather non-descript two story concrete block structure with large viewing windows on the upper level and baggage collection facilities on the ground level. The adjacent buildings and the control tower, positioned around the tarmac, were of the same block construction. There didn't seem to be any provisions for night landings, neither runway lights nor beacons.

Once on the ground, Al stopped Angela, the flight attendant.

"Do you not have any night landings at all?"

"Oh, yes, Senor Provo. We put out lit oil-filled flare pots and say many prayers."

The cabin door was opened and a gust of oxygen-starved air invaded the cabin. Unfortunately, the local odors of unleashed garbage and human waste came with the influx of air. These odors would remain a constant during his stay in Bolivia.

The passengers climbed down the rolling stairs to de-plane, then walked along the faded painted lines to the terminal.

Al climbed off the plane slowly, walking down a roll-up stairway. He made his way through to Baggage Claim, his ears still vibrating from the churning of the Pratt & Whiney engines on the old DC-7. Looking at his watch, he realized that it was indeed already Saturday morning.

CHAPTER 5

Bob Adams had arrived at the job site at an early hour for a meeting with the Canadian Engineer Pty. Ltd. group to discuss their mutual problem. The meeting was made up of the principals of the engineers' crew.

The Resident Engineer was Pierre Lamont, originally from Montreal, where he had graduated from McGill University. In his early forties, Lamont was a rigorous energetic outdoor type, easily 6' tall. He was a blond French Canadian, impatience being his demeanor. He had arrived in Bolivia as a bachelor, and nothing concrete was known of his past, other than he has worked for the same engineering company for fifteen years: Canadian Engineers Pty. Ltd.

The Assistant Resident Engineer was Ian MacDonald, from Toronto, a dark haired Scot working his first overseas project. He was squarely built, but reasonably even tempered.

Francois LaBatt was the Chief Inspector for the engineer. He was a suave 5'8" slender olive-skinned import from the Quebec City area. Francois sported a well groomed thin Perot type black mustache that he often tweaked as he spoke. He was rather aloof in dealing with anyone other than Pierre Lamont. Labatt claimed to have a degree in engineering from MaGill University. He, too, was a bachelor, and seemed to pride himself in the distinction of being quite a ladies' man. Labatt was vain and tended to fly off the handle when crossed by anyone. He had a very guarded past and turned the subject whenever anyone asked him where he worked or lived before coming to Bolivia.

Pierre asked, "Bob, can you tell us any more about your plans to get the TBM moving and the work back on schedule?"

"Well, yes, I can now truthfully say that one of the BOSCO top tunnel people will arrive here today. He has many miles of tunnel work behind him, specifically, bored tunnels in all kinds of rock. I asked that he be sent to back me up on this problem," replied Bob.

"What's his name? Can you give me some data on him? What are his credentials?" asked Pierre.

"His name is Albert Provo, and here is his resume. I have never worked with him but I am led to believe that he can be a real hard ass if that is what it takes. I would expect that with his world wide connections he probably has a full report on the history of everyone on the job including me. I also hear that he is the kind that looks, listens, and then he acts. Any questions?" asked Bob.

LaBatt's knuckles turned white as did his face. "Is he a cop?"

"No, not that I know of. Why? Don't you like cops?"queried Bob.

"That is not the point, I just don't trust them," replied LaBatt.

Francois thought to himself for a moment: "I'll have to walk easy around this guy, may even have to postpone getting into the contractor's pocket. If he gets too close, I may have to change my plans."

In actuality, Francois LaBatt was born in Montreal in 1930 to a single mother of dubious morals, in the slum area of the city. He was raised on the streets as his mother chased him out of the single room she inhabited whenever she had a customer. He learned to pimp, to steal, and to make book for the Mafia. His second home was a local saloon in the harbor area of Montreal. He found that he could pick a pocket and hide the goods under the thick layers of sawdust that covered the floor. His specialty was cleaning out the pockets of passed out wharfies and sailors that inhabited the area.

He managed to escape the notice of the law in the neighborhood, but when he was ten, he was picked up and sent to a reformatory. It did not take many beatings by inmates and guards before he learned to keep a very low profile. He was a quick study and soon found that he could do much better if he were educated. He put on the face of the poor little boy who was struggling to make something of himself. He eventually gained a vocation in construction and one way or another worked his way up to the job of construction inspector on major projects.

Bob looked at his watch.

"We'll break for now. I'm headed toward the airport to pick up Mr. Provo. We should all be prepared for some hard work Monday morning."

And with that declaration, Bob nodded to his group and walked briskly out the door, already thinking about the 45-minute drive down the mountain to meet Al Provo.

CHAPTER 6

An hour later, Al was deciding that he would take time to grab a quick cup of coffee, to tide him over until he got to the hotel. Pulling the travel packet from his coat pocket, he was trying to find the name of the hotel when he heard a loud throat-clearing sound from behind him.

"Are you Al Provo?" a gruff voice queried.

"Yes, and who might you be?" Al asked, looking at a younger man in his thirties.

"I'm Bob Adams. I got a message from BOSCO headquarters that you were on your way here."

Al remembered hearing that Robert Adams was the project manager on the Trans Andean Hydro Tunnel Project. He had arrived in Bolivia with his wife Agnes, two daughters, Rita and Sarah, as well as two sons, John and Raymond. He had an engineering degree and spoke fluent Spanish, French, and was learning Quechua. He had bid and completed two major tunnel and hydro projects for BOSCO in the past eight years. He was an avid hunter and fisherman as well as being completely devoted to his wife and children.

He has been known to attend stand-up cocktail parties and to be very able to keep up with the other party goers. Bob was widely known to be a no nonsense manager, strict but fair to the extreme. Ten to twelve hour days were his norm. He, however, lacked direct experience with Tunnel Boring Machines. The TBM on this project was a first in Bolivia.

Al looked over his soon-to-be working partner. For the first time since he left California, Al felt at ease about the upcoming project.

"Good to be here, Bob."

Bob quickly sized up the man in front of him. Al's reputation had preceded him. Bob knew that Albert Provo was forty, an American construction trouble shooter for BOSCCO. But Bob also noted the crew cut blond hair, the 6 foot, 190 pound muscular build. He had heard that Al claimed to be descended from French Canadian, Abenaki Indian, and Pennsylvania German ancestors as well as Scots and Irish. Bob knew that Al was reasonably fluent in both French and Spanish.

Bob matched Al's pace as they left the airport.

"I hear that you served in the airborne infantry during the Korea peace actions from 1951 to 1953 as a platoon leader. Korea was a bitch, wasn't it? How did you manage to get into doing tunnel projects after your discharge?"

"Oh, I guess I got into some 'difficult situations,' shall we say? Over in Korea, that is. Next thing I knew, somebody up the ladder had promoted me to Project Manager on several small tunnel projects in the Rocky Mountains."

What Bob didn't know was that Al's assignment to troubleshoot the problems plaguing the Trans-Andean Hydro Tunnel Project was destined to test Al's ability to cope not only with adversity but to show his knack of improvisation in areas other than tunnels. The second part of the assignment had been at the request of the CIA, who being the secretive organization that they are did not bother to let him know why they wanted him in Bolivia. "That would come later, much later," Al hoped, "on a need to know basis."

Al was also sizing up Bob, as they left the airport, going out into the glaring Bolivian sunshine.

Bob also sported a blond crew cut. He looked like he was in excellent physical health, ready to take on anything or anybody that got in his way. His green eyes looked piercingly at Al, weighing him up, making an on the spot assessment as to whether he would be of any help to him or if his reputation was all bull crap.

"Just so you understand," said Bob. "I asked for you to be sent here to help me out of this mess. You have a lot more experience with Tunnel Boring Machines (TBMs) and bad ground than I do. So! Welcome to the end of the world, let's grab your bags and head for the hotel while I brief you on the problems."

"A lot you know," thought Al.

With that, Bob grabbed one of Al's bags and started for the waiting 4x4, to be greeted by his driver. Al handed his other bag to the driver and climbed in the back of the 4x4 Suburban with Bob.

They started toward town on a gravel paved road. The road passed by a junk yard, surrounded by a high wood fence, a construction company equipment yard, protected by a high stone wall topped with barbed wire and broken glass. They drove past the local red light district of Cochabamba, housed in a two story dilapidated building.

"Is this the high rent district of Cochabamba?" Al smiled.

They started driving by low rent housing and eventually into the business district and the Main Plaza.

The basic color of the buildings along the streets was either yellow or faded red. The buildings all appeared to be of adobe brick stucco construction. Most of the houses were two story flat roofed structures with a low parapet surrounding the roof.

All the residences had eight foot high stone or brick walls surrounding the property. The stone walls all were topped with either broken glass concreted into the top of the wall or barbed wire along the tops. Some had both the glass and the barbed wire. All of the properties had large solid looking iron gates with secure locks to prevent entry to unwanted people. The yards were protected by yapping dogs ranging from small noisy ones to very large hungry ones.

"Are those walls and barbed wire there to keep the inhabitants in or the riff-raff out?" asked Al with serious grin.

The prevailing stench was either abating or his sense of smell had taken a holiday.

Al first noticed the rolling wreck of a truck when he heard the constant backfiring of the engine and the roar of the worn out muffler. He did note that one of the truck tires looked like it had a very big patch that bumped along as the truck bounced down the street.

Bob grinned and said, "If the driver has a blowout that breaks through the tire sidewall, the normal mode of repair is to cut a piece of tire from a junked tire, about a foot and a half long, and wire it to the outside of the defective tire on the truck, covering the blowout. This of course requires a new inner tube. It seems to work as there are many such repairs bumping up and down the local streets and roads."

Al thought to himself that Bob was unusually observant, as he had picked up on Al's frowning at the truck tires. "I need to play it very close to the vest until I have a good handle on the situation down here," Al mused silently.

"Bob, I was told that you have a TBM trapped by a rock fall. What's being done to save the TBM and backup floor?" Al asked as they drove into town.

"We were able to get all of the miners out of the tunnel within a few hours of the rock fall. The TBM is a different matter. We can get to that problem on Monday when we get to the job site. You have to see it to believe it. The basic problems are unskilled labor trying to work with space age equipment, and space age equipment being used in a Stone Age environment."

"Can you describe this TBM to me? We did not have any particulars about the machine in our files in San Francisco?" asked Al.

"The TBM has twenty four 12-inch diameter rotary cutter disks mounted on its fourteen-foot diameter cutter head. Each disk weighs 300 pounds. The cutter head weighs 75 tons while the rest of the machine, including four electric motors that rotate the cutter head at 2.5 RPM, weighs another 125 tons. The control, or driver's console, is just behind the cutter head and under the material conveyor. A structural steel frame supports the conveyor and the track way for the muck cars. The overall length of this $6,000,000 machine is 150 feet. The whole unit is powered by 3200 volts carried in a 3" diameter power cable. The TBM was delivered to the site in many small pieces, and assembled in place," explained Bob, just like he was teaching a class.

Bob had defined his problems rather succinctly, but probably more completely than Al would have. This being Saturday morning, Bob suggested that Al should book into the Hotel Vista Tunari, take a short nap, and then join him and his wife for a late lunch on the Prado.

"I'll be by to meet you about 2 PM. Remember, we are on hora Boliviana, so nothing moves like it does at home."

Al grabbed his gear from the car, but instantly had it taken over by a young boy who looked to be in his early teens. Defensively, Al wrenched his two bags away, stuffed some coins in the boy's hand, and turned back to grin at Bob.

"See you tonight, Bob. Thanks for the lift."

Al walked slowly into the hotel. He knew he was being paranoid about his luggage, but he had learned the hard way that no one, not any person, need ever touch his personal bags. He tried to relax as he came into the coolness of the hotel lobby.

The lobby reminded him of some of the old hotels he had lived in, in the mid west. It was rather ornate with tapestries on the walls and genuine but well worn Persian rugs on the wood floors. The paint was a bit tired but had not yet started to peel off the walls.

"I can't say that I really like the grey and yellow décor, but after all I'm only going to sleep here and not buy the place," thought Al.

The creaky old elevator groaned and grumbled at having to raise itself up three floors.

"This elevator must have been a reject from the Arc."

Al remembered that in this part of the world the third floor becomes number two as the first floor is called the ground level. The wood paneling looked tired and could have used a new coat of varnish. The wood floor badly needed re-painting. The lobby and hallways smelled of Lysol and mold.

The hall leading to room #233 was rather dark, being lighted by an occasional 40 watt bulb that seemed to wink at him as the current changed from 60, down to 40 cycles, and back up again. Al knew he would soon find that the variation in electrical power ran the gamut between 110 and 220 volts several times daily, depending on the power drain at that instant in time.

The door to his room looked like it had been opened way too many times and needed new hardware as well as paint. The room was rather spacious, with a wide wooden board floor covered with throw rugs. The floor creaked as he walked around the room. The furniture was rather nondescript, but utilitarian. Al thought he would need to invest in a flashlight, as the single 40 watt bulb in the one ceiling fixture was not very bright.

All in all, the room and the bath room all appeared reasonably clean, in spite of the slight scent of musk and mold. There was a tinge of some rather strange perfume that he could not place. Al refrained from opening the window, first to reduce the risk of someone sneaking in while he slept, but more to avoid the influx of the local odors. He had not been there long enough to become immune to the collective odors of Bolivian society, but he remembered. The smell of this country could not be forgotten.

Al could hear the constant roar of tired out old motors and the slamming of an occasional car door at the front of the hotel. The collectivos (busses) rattled up and down the street at irregular intervals. Occasionally he could pick out the tell tale sound of an old Ford V-8 flat-head engine. That brought back many good memories. The taxis were mostly vintage cars of the late thirties to the mid fifties.

Al saw a number of 1938 Fords, 1949 Chevrolets and an occasional 1940 Plymouth. They had all apparently started work in Bolivia, climbing the hills of LaPaz until the strain overtook their running gear. They were then shipped to Cochabamba with its nearly flat plain. Many of them had been modified and now were propelled by diesel engines.

They were all the worse for wear but at least their tires did not have the supplemental external patches.

Looking at his watch, Al quickly calculated that he could indeed catch a much-needed short nap. Shedding rumpled clothes quickly, he was soon deep into sleep.

He didn't fear over-sleeping. Part of Al's constitution was his ability to set his internal alarm clock. It never failed him. He woke up an hour later and decided he might as well get dressed and wait for Bob in the hotel bar.

CHAPTER 7

There were other arrivals to Cochabamba that day.

Al walked into the hotel bar intent upon squandering an hour until Bob Adams arrived at 2:00 PM. He settled on a bar stool and looked over at Peter, the gringo bartender, and asked, "Do you have any good Scotch, not that potato whiskey you get from Argentina?"

With a wise grin Peter replied, "Hey, if you have the money, I have the best Scotch you can buy in Cochabamba." He poured a good tumbler full of Glenfidich, threw in a couple of ice cubes and handed it to Al. "That will be five dollars, American."

"How did you know?" Al smiled.

"Easy. I could make up something, but I saw you dealing with our local baggage-boy. He meant no harm, but I could tell you wanted a quick hands-off from him. You don't look like a tourist."

Well, you don't look like a Bolivian bartender. Guess no one is who he looks like, right?"

And with that Al threw down the rest of his Scotch, and shoved the glass toward Peter. They grinned at each other. Peter quickly filled his glass again with warm liquor and ice cubes.

Al sat swirling his Scotch on the rocks on the bar top when he smelled a very interesting perfume permeating the fan blown air. He looked around to see a very nice looking woman maybe in her thirties, sitting at a nearby table all by her lonesome. She was a petite brunet, dressed in a shear blue blouse and white pleated skirt that showed off her figure to great advantage. She wore dangling earrings that matched her blouse, an enormous diamond, and a most remarkably beautiful smile. Al rather doubted that the smile was for him, as she looked up and motioned to a tall blond good looking thirty something man in a business suit who had just come into the room. He nodded to Al as he walked by to her table. They embraced and sat down for another drink.

George leaned over to Patricia, and in a barely audible voice said, "That American might be our contact. Why don't we invite him over, then we can find out?"

George beckoned to Al to join them. Al slid off his bar stool and walked over to their table.

"Hi, I'm George Jordan and this is my wife, Patricia," George said.

Al took a second to look George over, then Patricia, before he responded.

"Al Provo. I'm a tourist here in Bolivia."

"You look like a new arrival in Cochabamba. Have you had time to get used to the altitude?" Patricia queried. She reached out her hand to touch Al's.

"I do seem to have a little problem breathing if I run up the stairs too fast," smiled Al.

"You seem to have acclimated rather well, though." Patricia almost seemed to be issuing some kind of invitation to Al.

George interjected, "We're in LaPaz for a week, so we're pretty well used to the altitude here. Patricia, I do think that we should go on up to our room and unpack, don't you? Please excuse us, Mr. Provo. We'll see you later."

George and Patricia stood up, almost as one person. Al couldn't know that, without saying any words out loud, they had decided Al was not the one they were to meet.

Dressed as stylishly as they were, Al felt they were possibly tourists just arrived in Bolivia, but they also had other reasons for their travels. Were they possibly avoiding something or someone in their home country? He had the feeling that they had thought he was someone they were here to meet, but had missed.

*

George and Patricia walked slowly into their shared room to discuss their next move.

They knew they had to make contact with someone here in Bolivia that might be able to give them information on Franco BonNuit.

"He wasn't our contact, so we have to keep a reasonably low profile," stated George. They had to make certain with their information as to the identity of the man. There were a number of Canadians in Bolivia.

"We have an old photo of him, but we need more than that. Our mission is to find and apprehend Franco BonNuit one way or another." said Patricia. "Remember what Inspector Gagnon told us before we left Montreal. The Canadian police are most anxious to apprehend him."

"Don't forget our smiling friend, the Godfather of the French Mafia in Quebec, Don Antonio. He told us that BonNuit is a French Canadian who angered the French Mafia in Quebec by first scamming them out of a large sum of money and then by turning them over to the Quebec Serrate. He angered them so much that the Mafia is offering $1,000,000 for Bon Nuit, preferably dead. I don't feel he was kidding."

Both George and Patricia had served in the Canadian armed forces in intelligence and   police units. They were both fluent in three languages. Patricia was an expert long range marksman, a back up on the Canadian Olympic long range rifle team.

The two of them had been always worked as a team. Their home base was Montreal, Quebec, Canada. They had been very effective, in that they had a success rate of above 90%. They had formed a team as youngsters and continued working together. They traveled extensively following leads as to the whereabouts and identity of their quary.

CHAPTER 8

Several miles away, Bob was smiling to himself. He had a natural instinct for people, and already felt comfortable around this Al Provo. He stood in front of the closet, decided to change jackets, and grabbed the first one he saw.

Bob was walking out of his bedroom, putting on a navy-colored jacket when Agnes saw him.

"Where are you going all dressed up, got a date?" she bantered.

"No, I've actually already been to the airport, straight from work, to pick up the guy from the States who's come down to help us with the TBM."

Agnes nodded. Bob started telling her last week about the trouble shooter from California.

"So he'll be the one to help get the tunnel moving again?" Agnes asked.

Last night Bob couldn't stop talking about Al Provo, the American construction trouble shooter. Bob said that Al had served in the airborne infantry in Korea in the early 1950s as a platoon leader. But Agnes also was surprised that Bob seemed to know that this engineer was said to have been in the OSS and had spent a lot of time behind enemy lines.

"You know, Agnes," quickly said Bob, "you would like this Al fellow. He's quite charming and apparently has a great reputation with the ladies. Wouldn't you like to go with him to introduce him to our charming little town?"

"Well, okay. Give me about five minutes, and I'll be ready. Always willing to meet new men."

And with that, she leaned into him, giving him one of their special kisses.

True to his word, Bob and his charming wife Agnes arrived at the hotel at the designated time.

*

Al was waiting for them inside the hotel. He was instantly focused on the woman at Bob's side. She was a petite blond bundle of effervescent energy, with a mesmerizing smile for everyone. Her bright blue eyes looked straight into his and defied him to try to tell her anything but the truth.

All Al knew was that she seemed very young to be the mother of four. She was dressed in tan form-fitting slacks and a white blouse with embroidered flowers. Her hair was coiffed in short waves.

"I am so glad to meet you at last. Did you have a good flight down here? Bob says that you are here to help him get the TBM back to work. We expect you to be our guest at dinner and social happenings while you're in Cochabamba. I won't take no for an answer either. Bob may be Project Manager on the tunnel but I'm the head knocker at home. OK?"

They went out from the Main Plaza to a four lane street divided by a 75 feet wide park down the center. The wind was strong enough here to dissipate the odors of garbage and human waste to a cloying reminder that, though the smell had somewhat deployed, it was still there.

This section was known as the Prado, a nicely landscaped park with trees and flowers. Several water fountains were strategically placed at either end of the park. A paved sidewalk traversed both sides of the park along the roadway. A cleanup crew armed with palm fronds swept away any debris on the sidewalks. The sides of these lanes were occupied by many mom-and-pop stores and eateries. These were primarily on the lower floor while living quarters were on the upper level. The private residences were mostly two story flat roofed dwellings surrounded by high barbed wire and glass topped walls. They stopped at a sidewalk café that specialized in beer and sultanas, folded pastries filled with meat, gravy, and vegetables, similar to a meat turnover.

"There's a really nice cocktail party tonight at the Consulate and you're invited to attend. You'll meet a number of single and not so single young ladies there that are very interested in meeting you," Agnes informed Al.

"The altitude may affect your consumption of alcohol, but then we will make certain that you don't get into too much trouble. I hope you understand that the Bolivian clocks move at a different pace than ones in the US. If you are invited to a dinner at, say, 7:00 PM, you'll find that most of the guests won't arrive until closer to 8:00 PM. This is the notorious hora Boliviana," Agnes continued.

"OK, Agnes, have you been on the phone again?" huffed Bob. "I suppose you told all the single women that Al is single."

"Well, you know how the ladies, and the Women's Club, all want to know about any newcomers to Cochabamba. They want to be sure that they have all the latest gossip," she smirked.

They finished their lunch, and as they were ready to leave, a dark haired beauty approached their table.

Bob introduced Al to Margarita Suarez. "Al, this beautiful lady and her husband are two of our favorite party friends."

Maggie looked Al over like a hungry leopardess eyeing its next meal. She saw a very fit, good looking crew cut blonde with deep blue eyes that did not appear to miss anything, even to the curves of her well formed body.

"So! This is the new man in town. Please call me Maggie. Will I be seeing you at the party this evening? I would not want to miss that. There'll be a lot of nice young single women there that are interested in meeting you - that is if I don't kidnap you first. Ta! Ta! I have to run. Be seeing you guys later."

"Just be warned, Al, she is married, but is predatory and tries to latch onto any new man in town," Bob remarked quietly, hoping that Agnes had not heard him.

"Don't start spreading rumors," said Agnes, obviously listening to everything Bob had said.

Agnes went on to ask if Al would come to their place on the Prado for dinner at seven before going on to the party.

Being an astute politician, he immediately said yes. "I'll catch a taxi and be there in my dress up clothes."

After all, who would want to miss a good home cooked meal, he thought to himself. Home cooked food should always take precedence over politics.

Al had been living out of restaurants most of his life. Besides, he needed to get to know the Adams family better, as he would be working with them for the next few months.

CHAPTER 9

He went back to the Hotel Vista Tunari by taxi. It cost all of 50 cents.

He unpacked his bags and hung his clothes in the old walnut armoire. Al saved out a clean set of underwear and socks and a handkerchief. After showering under an intermittent flow of cold, then hot water, he dressed in a pair of grey slacks, a figured cowboy shirt with the snap buttons, and a bolo tie of silver and turquoise. He donned his dark blue blazer and headed for the lobby. The taxi dropped him at the Adam's doorstep right at seven.

"None of this hora Boliviana for me," Al thought.

Agnes met Al at the door and was all smiles as she introduced her four children. "The eldest one is Rita, she is fourteen and already a very grown up young lady. Sarah is eleven."

Sarah was still at the awkward age, not at all sure of what or who she was. The boys, John at eight and Raymond at five, were all arms and legs. They were not particularly awed by Al's appearance in Bolivia; in fact, he was an interruption to their play with their neighbors' children.

Agnes went on to tell Al that Rita, Sarah, and John all attended the Institute Americano, a Methodist-sponsored institution of learning. They enrolled children from the 1st grade through to 12th grade. All classes were in Castellano (Castilian), except for the class in English.

Raymond attended the Hebrew Kindergarten. All the children had suffered through a Castilliian tutor since arriving and seemed to fall very quickly into speaking Castilliian. The girls were studying French, which they spoke with a Castilliian accent. The boys were learning Quechua from their school chums. Unfortunately John was losing his ability to spell in English, and Raymond not only spoke English, Quechua and Castilliian, but usually spoke all three jumbled together. The three older ones took horseback riding from a German equestrian teacher every Saturday. They did manage to learn to post under the very strict supervision of their instructor.

Al tried to take in everything Agnes was telling him, but he could tell the four children wanted nothing more than to be dismissed to their own devices.

"Glad to meet you, all of you." Al flashed them his biggest smile.

And with those words they vanished.

"They certainly have adapted well to living in a new country. I hope I do as well down here. Maybe they'll give me some pointers."

Agnes beamed. Al could tell that she was very proud of her children.

"Let's go into dinner, shall we?" And Agnes grabbed him by the arm and into the dining room they stepped.

They sat down to dinner served by the family cook. There was no green salad. Al soon learned that it was too difficult to separate the greens from the multitude of bugs in the country. All leafy foods had to be drowned in a potassium permanganate solution to dislodge the resident bugs. The beef was a filet that had been over cooked, also to kill off the bugs. Al was told that any other cut of beef was so tough that you could not chew it. The peas tasted like they were canned, another overcooked dish.

But then the bowl of fresh cooked red cabbage was passed to Al. One mouthful and he knew it was the best he'd ever had. Agnes told him the Bolivian cook was raised in a German family and had learned to cook a number of German dishes. The dessert was a very good German chocolate cake. They had a medium Chilean Chardonnay wine with dinner. The after-dinner drink was an excellent Spanish sherry.

They chatted for a while then left for the cocktail party, making sure that they did not arrive before the hora Boliviana, 9:30 pm, rather than the designated time of 9:00 pm. Even though they were tardy by thirty minutes they were still the third group to arrive.

As the evening wore on he met Father Tim, a Maryknoll priest; the US Consul, George Thomas; and, once again, was introduced to Margarita Saurez, and her husband Juan Saurez. He also met Major Wood and Major Wolf of the U.S. Special Forces Mission to Bolivia, and possibly twenty other people whose names became lost to him in complete confusion.

Major Wood looked somewhat familiar, so Al walked over to him and suggested that he thought he knew him.

The Major said, "You should know me because we were in jump school together at Fort Benning in 1951. We both joined the army in September 1950. We went on to the 90 day wonder school (OCS) together after jump school. I nearly lost track of you after that as I volunteered for the re-organized Rangers. How did you manage to get your butt out of North Korea after you and your team liberated those POW's? I heard that you had gone over to the Company doing black ops. I'll be calling on you one of these days soon, probably before the end of the week to give you a heads up on this mission."

Al shrugged his shoulders and smiled.

The Major had gone on to a new ranger battalion and ended up Special Forces after Korea. The more that he had to drink, the more humorous his stories about evading water buffalo in Vietnam became. Al laughed until his jaw started to lock up.

Al asked Bob, "How many different languages do they speak at this party? I think I recognized Castilliian, French, German, Hungarian and Quechua. Am I close?"

"You hit right on," said Bob.

He drifted over to the group around Juan Saurez, listening to him telling several people about himself. Al quickly found out that Saurez had studied engineering in the United States, later returning to Bolivia and his family roots. His family was among the early Spanish settlers in Bolivia. They had been forcibly removed from their extensive land holdings during the Agrarian Reform (MNR) of 1952. Juan's father was the oldest living Civil Engineer in Bolivia. He somehow assumed the managing of the local brewery.

Juan was more interested in his mistress than he was in his wife. That was the macho way in the days of his growing up and he could see little reason to change. He was in his late thirties, a dark complexioned handsome five foot eight Latin lover.

Al had met Maggie this afternoon and since had learned a bit more about her through local gossip. She was Juan's neglected wife, of French ancestry, a slim brunet all of five foot four at 120 pounds. She was wearing a form fitting dress that showed more of her than is normally thought to be modest. In fact, most of the male attendees at the party were having trouble keeping their gaze above her shoulders. The wives and girl friends seemed to have problems detracting their significant others to more modest activities. She was attracting the interest of most of the men. It would have been improper to say that she was promiscuous, however. Maggie just seemed to enjoy having a great number of very good men friends. Flirting had become a game with her. She tended to lead guys on, but no one was saying just how far she would go.

Al felt his arm being grasped and in a slight haze realized that it was Maggie tugging him toward another group of people. Among that group were her husband Juan and Father Tim. Juan did not have much to say as his attention was on Agnes who in return was doing her best to ignore his hitting on her.

Al did notice that Maggie was getting very chummy with a dark complexioned Latino engineer from Texas name Raul Majia. He apparently was a sales representative for electrical equipment, and did seem to appreciate Maggie's attributes. This apparently resulted in nothing more than a flirtation.

CHAPTER 10

Father Tim was a Maryknoll priest from upper North Dakota. He was about five foot nine inches tall and weighed 160 lbs. His salt and pepper hair was cut nearly to a crew cut style. He had divested himself of his priestly vestments and was dressed in a pair of grey slacks topped by an Izod tee shirt. He looked very much at ease with a tall glass of Scotch on the rocks in his left hand.

Father Tim and Al hit it off immediately. He told how he had been assigned to the parish of San Pablo 15 years ago. He had let his feelings be known to the local Communist party leaders. The local Communists had beaten him badly, leaving him with a very un-Christian attitude toward them.

They swilled down more than their fair share of free booze with both of them becoming rather talkative. Between drinks and nibbles, Father Tim and Al discussed the state of the world, abortion, and birth control in third world nations. They did not resolve anything, but by the end of the evening they were doing very well just to be able to stand up. Their friendship would grow over the next few months. He finally realized that Al was not about to convert to a Catholic. In doing so he told Al a few of his experiences since being appointed pastor of his flock.

One of his more interesting stories was that of his first few months at his new parish. Father Tim leaned back in the chair out on the veranda, took a sip of his drink, and began talking – not just to Al, but almost musing to himself. "My parish was made up of cholas from the pueblo of San Pablo. They were primarily poor transplanted campesinos who eked out a meager existence doing odd jobs and selling what ever goods they could beg borrow or steal. Some of their goods were obtained from the syndicato de las contrabandistas (smugglers union).

"The local women were easily identified from those of other parts of the Andes by their white stovepipe hats embellished by black ribbons. They all wore ponchos of varying colors and levels of disrepair. The women wore any number of flowered billowing skirts that were rotated from an inner layer as the outside garment became intolerably soiled. They mostly were barefoot or at times wore zapatos (sandals) made from old rubber tires.

"The men were dressed a bit differently in that their shirts were home spun, as were their trousers. They were firmly convinced that bathing would wash the protective layer of dirt from their bodies and would then allow illness. Consequently, gringos with even a poor sense of smell found that it was not desirable to be in close contact with the locals. This aversion seemed to wear off after a few months exposure.

"The one thing that did not wear off or go away was the continual parade of the hungriest fleas that I have ever had the misfortune of encountering. Not only were they very hungry, but they were Olympic jumpers even against a forty mile per hour head wind.

"The majority of the cholas homes were about fifteen by twenty feet one story structures made of sun baked mud blocks, dirt floors and thatched roofs. Some of the more wealthy ones had tile roofs. Sanitation was unheard of in small pueblos (towns) like San Pablo. This added to the stench in that area. They all had high walls surrounding them so that pigs, chickens and sheep could be kept close at hand.

"The first Sunday that I stood up to give mass I noticed that on the left side of the altar was a fully saddled and girdled horse with the old silver and gold Conquistador regalia. Sitting astride the horse was a fully fitted out Conquistador in all his magnificent silver and gold embossed body armor. As I preached my sermon and performed the mass, I was rather appalled to note that the cholas were not watching me but rather were staring at the Conquistador. I felt that possibly my sermon was not of sufficient substance to interest the parish.

"I remember working extra hard on my sermon for the next Sunday and had the exact same reaction from the cholas. After about a month of this non-attention to my sermons, I decided that the horse and rider had to go. The problem was that there was no door on the left side of the altar, only on the right side. I knew that all hell would break loose if I moved the offending horse and rider out post-haste. I did the sneaky thing. Each week I would move the horse and rider about a foot to the right until I was eventually able to push it out the door. All the time that I was doing this I watched the eyes of the worshipers follow the gradual retreat of the horse and conquistador."

This story told Al a lot about Father Tim. As Al's grandmother (WASP) would have said, "he's a nice guy, for a Catholic." The two of them started talking about some of the old Inca legends of such places as Incayacta. They suggested to each other that if they had the opportunity, they should check them out.

A second Maryknoll priest made an appearance. This was Father Sean McKenny. Father Sean was a younger man in his late twenties, very good looking (too good looking for a priest) and quite athletic. He had a liking for good Scotch and for sports such as hand ball and touch football.

"How would you like a good game of hand ball," Father Sean asked.

Al took the bait and smiled as he said," I would like to play, do you have any good players here in Cochabamba?" Al had forgotten that he was now 8500 feet above sea level with the corresponding reduction of the oxygen in the air.

Al took him up on that game a few evenings later. He found that the good Fathers all knew cuss words that he had never even heard from miners. They not only had extensive vocabularies, but were all world class players.

Al wasn't sure he had ever played quite so hard. His hands were scraped and cut. His heart seemed to be ready to burst out of his chest at any time during the game, but what a game.

A week later, after his hands had healed, he joined in a game of touch football. It took him nearly two weeks to heal up from that contest.

"This isn't touch football, it's hard tag and tackle football. I had not believed that priests were all that intent upon mayhem, unless he had misunderstood this not as football but as an inquisition with all its tortures?" murmured Al as he limped back to his hotel.

Al left the party somewhere around 2:00AM with Bob and Agnes. They dropped him off at the hotel after making him promise to be at their house for dinner Sunday afternoon.

"I don't want to mooch free meals off you guys and wear out my welcome," Al said, hoping they wouldn't really be convinced.

Agnes replied, "We have too few visitors from home to be anything but grateful for a new face."

"Well, thank you, I'm always glad to miss hotel or restaurant food."

Al had little trouble getting to sleep. It had been days, or so he felt, since he'd had a good night's sleep. He was rudely awakened about an hour later by gun fire. The sound of a BAR (Browning automatic rifle) down in the street in front of the hotel. About then a Grease Gun (.45 caliber) popped off a half dozen rounds to the accompaniment of a German Burp Gun (9 mm). This occurred three times in the following hour. Al could not go to sleep for some time. He was in a cold sweat recalling the last time he had heard those weapons being fired. That had been during a military operation in Vietnam while the French Foreign Legion was still in control. He had been sent there to extract an American

DICK ROBERTS

VIP who had been in the wrong place at the wrong time and had been captured by the insurgents.

CHAPTER 11

Sunday morning, actually nearly afternoon, after recovering from the rather liquid and noisy evening the previous night, Al showered and shaved, dressed in his casual slacks and shirt, then went down to the lobby looking for breakfast. The desk clerk directed him to the dining room. He had learned the hard way that an excess of alcohol and high altitudes do not blend well.

"Buenas Dias Senor, Como esta? (Good morning sir, how are you?) Would you care for breakfast?" the head waiter asked.

"Yes, I would like some strong black coffee, orange juice and ham and eggs, scrambled, thank you."

Al soon found that strong black coffee in Bolivia was indeed strong. Strength-wise, strong black coffee in Bolivia seemed to be just a hair below varnish remover. It was almost strong enough to melt the enamel on his teeth. He had a feeling he would learn to enjoy it before he left Bolivia.

He ate a leisurely breakfast, and then decided to see what Cochabamba looked like. The center of the city was a large square with a park in the center.

The Main Plaza was typical of Spanish urban design of 300 years ago. A wide walkway fronted all the buildings with the exception of the church. The walkway was covered by the overhang of the upper stories of the buildings. The overhang was fronted by gracious arches and hanging baskets of flowers.

A large ornate Catholic church dominated one side of the square while the three remaining sides were made up of stores and cafes. The church was of granite while the remaining buildings were stucco over either adobe or granite blocks.

Al noted that there were soldiers on all of the roofs of surrounding buildings, manning machine guns. There were a large number of armed military around the Main Plaza. He later heard that there had been some threats of rioting scheduled for this morning.

There were clothing stores, hardware stores, meat markets and general grocery stores, some with produce. Opposite the Catholic Church were the police station and the city offices. This was also the location of the

Alcaldes office. These buildings all had large atriums surrounded by offices.

Traffic was haphazardly directed by brown uniformed traffic police. Al knew he was taking his life in his hands when he started across the street. He was later told never to give his drivers license to a traffic policeman. It would cost him about $10.00 to get it back.

The city was laid out in squares so that all streets run parallel, either east and west or north and south. The streets running off the Main Plaza had streets more or less twenty feet wide, with sidewalks two to three feet wide running against the front of the buildings. The buildings rise up in vertical walls forming rather formidable canyons of off color red with heavily shuttered doors and windows. A great variety of stores line these side streets harboring clothing, hardware, pharmacies and meat markets. An occasional auto and or bicycle shop were also be found along the way. All of the stores were fitted out with iron grills over the doors and widows. The doors were all massive heavy timber, one way in, one way out. This reduced shoplifting. Al wandered into an electrical store that sold every imaginable electrical appliance from toasters to electric stoves and refrigerators.

The proprietor, Al later learned, had been liberated from the Nazi concentration camp at Auschwitz. Jacob Liebowitz had migrated to Sacramento, California, where he worked as a baker for a number of years. His brother had migrated to Cochabamba and started the electrical appliance store. After a very successful five years, the brother had convinced Jacob that his fortune was in Bolivia.

"Try it for five years, then you can go back to Sacramento a rich man," he had told Jacob.

Al met Jacob several months before he returned to Sacramento, indeed a rich man.

Al quickly learned he had to be on the alert against pickpockets, as that seemed to be a national pastime in Cochabamba. Not only was it the national pastime in Bolivia, but it seemed that Cochabamba was the national training school for them.

As he was walking along the street he saw a small crowd watching some poor devil lying on the sidewalk in the midst of an epileptic seizure. At the back of the crowd Al witnessed a pickpocket with his hand in the bag of a woman watching the seizure. The hand came out with the woman's pocket book. The pickpocket then dissolved into the crowd. No one said a word.

Al went back to the hotel and relaxed a bit before heading out to Bob and Agnes's home on the Prado. He learned that the local soccer stadium was about three blocks past the Adams' house on the Prado. He could hear the cheering crowds watching a soccer match.

CHAPTER 12

Al arrived at the Adams' household barely behind Father Tim and Father Sean. They had been there long enough to remove their collars and head for the bar in the kitchen for a whisky. A few minutes later an Anglican priest from Australia and his wife showed up. They found that they had many mutual friends in Australia. He had been assigned the parish in Cochabamba. He told Al that he had a problem with alcohol, therefore only drank sherry. Another interesting couple arrived with their two toddlers. They were the Jacobs, both missionaries for the Bolivian Baptist Ministry. They neither smoked nor drank alcoholic beverages, but seemed to be tolerant of those who did.

The next people to arrive were several Peace Corps volunteers from various places in the states. After nearly an hour of socializing, Agnes announced that dinner was being served and that they should sit down at the table for a belated New Year's meal, complete with a large roasted turkey, cranberry sauce and corn meal dressing. The mashed potatoes were smothered in turkey gravy. White Chilean wine and freshly squeezed orange juice completed the main course. For dessert they had fresas (strawberries) and whipped cream on short bread, and American coffee.

After dinner, stories were told during coffee. This had developed into a ritual after any meal with company. Agnes told Al about Bolivian Carnival (Mardi Gras). This celebration lasts for a week of intense partying and carousing with a masked ball on the last night. This was by invitation only as it sometimes evolved into assignations between various lovers, married or not. The Adams had declined this get together.

During the day the younger set threw water balloons at and into any automobiles that they could find driving up the street. It happened that Sarah Adams had a filled water balloon and was perched on top of the stone gate post in front of the house when she sighted a jeep with an open window. She threw the balloon quite accurately and placed it squarely in the jeep window. The jeep was a police vehicle. The occupants were not very happy. Sarah gave them a sickly broad smile, lept off the stone gate post, completely forgetting how to speak Castilliian and headed for the sanctuary of her home.

The dinner party ended about 9:00 PM when everyone, including Al, left to catch some rest for tomorrow, a work day.

Monday morning came, finally. Al knew he had postponed working on the project, but once he started, he would have to be on site for five and one half days per week. He would be commuting to work from town every day, so the average day would be about fourteen hours. What an infringement on his party time, he thought to himself, laughing. But he knew there was a love of the job that always kept him eager and ready whenever those plane tickets would land on his desk.

He ate a quick breakfast, a standard on his work days. Bob picked Al up at the hotel at six.

"We'll get you a vehicle and a driver this afternoon so you won't be so dependent on me," Bob said, as they were driving to the job.

Al commented, "The vista is intoxicating. The mountain peaks rise straight up into the cobalt blue sky. Occasionally a fluffy cloud drifted slowly by to relieve the potential monotony of the beauty that surrounded them."

They looked down two thousand feet to watch the low jungle clouds swirl in and out of the steep walled mountain canyons. They were surrounded by peaks that thrust their way up another five thousand feet like sentinels guarding them from the wrath of the ancient Inca gods. Some of these peaks pierced the sky at eighteen thousand feet. This was the Cordirilla Oriental of the High Andes. They could see the azure waters of the sterile mountain lakes nestled between the precipitous crags. The bare mountain slopes had been deprived of all vegetation other than a short wiry grass. Any trees that may have been there were long gone to provide heat for the campesinos.

Some of the slopes were heavily terraced to provide flat spaces for growing potatoes and corn. The campesinos burned off all the slopes above ten thousand feet to urge the grass to grow for feed for their sheep. It never came back with anything more than sparse widely spaced clumps that barely afforded fodder for a rabbit. A small grove of Eucalyptus had survived on the upper slopes. The rain forest topped out at the ten thousand foot level. Below that they found Mahogany and luxuriant under growth adorned by many different varieties of orchid and rhododendrons.

The highway was a gravel surfaced wash board, more or less 16 feet wide. The road had been perched on the near vertical mountain slopes, being at times as much as 500 feet above the floor of the canyon, and 300 to 700 feet below the top of the ridge. The curves were predominately blind hair pins with little or no sight distance for on coming vehicles.

The first one at the curve sounded his horn to warn on-coming cars or trucks of his approach. At night the locals drove without lights until they met another vehicle; then they turned on their high beams. The first one to turn on his lights had the right-of-way. This act resulted in everyone being blinded. The gringos all claimed that was so the drivers could not see who hit them.

CHAPTER 13

They arrived at the site in a little less than 45 minutes. The office was a one story unpainted timber building that had received very little assistance from an architect. The office sat about 10 feet above road grade, possibly to prevent local drivers from running into the front door. The single story grey mess hall was located on the far side of the road. The change house for the crew was another grey one story structure about a hundred yards down the road toward the tunnel portal. The compressor house and the repair shops were wedged in between the mess hall and the change house on a very narrow bench cut into the side of the mountain. The job warehouse was set next to the mess hall away from the other structures. The Engineer's office was set back up the hill about 50 yards above the construction office.

Bob and Al got out of the Suburban and went into the office. Al was introduced to Will Barret, the Project Engineer, and Alberto Lopez, the Office Engineer. Bob and Al walked into the Resident Engineer's office where Al was introduced to Pierre Lamont, the Resident Engineer, and his assistant, Ian MacDonald, both Canadians. They seemed glad to have someone on site that purported to know something about T.B.M.'s.

Back in the BOSCO office he met the office manager, Juan Batista, a former Bolivian Army Colonel who had been on the wrong side in the last revolution. He had just recently been allowed back into Bolivia. He had been exiled to Peru, in a system of reciprocity for revolutionaries. He was the brother-in-law of one of the late co-presidents.

Jesus Domingo was the general superintendent. Jesus was a Quechua Indian, about 6'0" tall and weighed in at 200 pounds. His height made him an exception to the normal male in Bolivia. Al suspected that he made superintendent the same way old time first sergeants made rank. They could whip everybody in the company. Jesus was dark complexioned with a lock of dark black hair falling under his hard hat. He had experience with earthwork, mining, rock quarrying and concrete, but none with TBM's. Al was told that he was a very able superintendent when he knew the work. Al was guessing that Jesus would require some on-the-job training on the TBM.

George Padilla was the master mechanic in charge of keeping the TBM running. It might have been a good guess that he was probably a good tractor mechanic, but it was believed that he was a fish out of water when it came to a TBM. Again, OJT (on the job training).

The one TBM operator was Pedro Vargas. His claim to fame was that he had operated heavy equipment for many years. Unfortunately, they would need one for each shift when they went to three shifts per day. More OJT was definitely required here.

Bob and Al along with Jesus and George went into the tunnel to orient Al as to the problems they had encountered. They met Pedro at the end of the backup floor.

The tunnel was a nominal 14'-0" diameter and would be 20,000 feet from portal to portal. The first 200 feet had been mined by drill and blast methods through badly decomposed rock. Steel ribs and wood lagging had been installed to keep the blocky rock from falling. The ribs had been set about 10 feet behind the TBM cutter head. The roof had fallen in about 20 feet behind the cutter head and had completely locked the machine in place. The rock in front of the machine had been test drilled and the drill cores indicated that it was going to be more of the same for a minimum of 150 feet on down the tunnel. To worsen the situation, a water flow of plus or minus 2000 gpm had started in the face. The water was a lubricant for the rock formations. This would provide some rather unstable ground as well as making all TBM rescue work very difficult.

Al climbed around and into openings in the rock fall until several large rock falls threatened to bury him.

"Get to hell out of there before you get yourself killed. I don't want to have to explain to the main office that you were making like a gopher on your first day on the job," yelled Bob.

"There is no better way to understand the problem than to become a part of the problem," Al explained in rather subdued tones. "Let's get back to the office where we can review the geology report by the designers."

They went back to the office and pulled the geological report out of the file. The drill cores had been stored in town, so they would have to go back down the hill to inspect those later. The geological report indicated that there should be massive moderately jointed rock starting within 100 feet of the portal. That is not what they had seen in the tunnel.

"Being slightly paranoid when viewing drill logs, I would suggest that we should check the actual drill cores in Cochabamba tomorrow to decide for ourselves as to whether the cores match the logs," commented Al.

The group spent the balance of the day reviewing the TBM maintenance records and the cutter head repair and maintenance procedures that were planned for the cutters and the machine.

They then approached the problem a bit more aggressively, trying to get some input from the crew. Barring that, Al decided to dive in head first.

"Bob, what do you think about driving a drift along the side of the machine so that we can access the cutter head? If we do that, we could drill ahead and grout off the water flow. That would allow us to reinforce the rock ahead of us until we find something stable. We can support the rock with rock bolts and shotcrete as well as timber ribs and timber lagging."

Al asked Bob and the general group in the room if they had any problems with that. All he got were vacant stares like a deer caught in headlights on a dark night.

He decided to let those thoughts gel overnight to see if he would get any reaction by the next day. He had always been of the opinion that you can't let a problem just sit there. It is better to do something even if it is wrong than to do nothing and let the lack of doing anything allow the problem to carve itself in granite.

CHAPTER 14

"Severeno over there with the Jeep will be at your disposal for as long as you want," Bob said as we were walking out of the office.

"And, one more thing, how about a drink at the house tonight so we can talk about this?"

"You know, Bob, that's exactly what I think we should do, providing you have some good Scotch, not that Argentine potato whiskey. I'll drop by about seven after I grab a bite at the hotel."

Al rode down the mountain with Severeno driving. It was dark out, so Severeno was driving with the headlights off. Al was not particularly thrilled with this as the road was only about 16 feet wide and dropped about 500 feet on the downhill side. No guard rails.

They met a truck coming up the hill. Then, Severeno turned on the high beams. That was when Al came unglued and pointedly informed him that he was to use headlights at night. Al didn't give a damn if it did run the battery down. Severeno did understand this, especially when he was presented with the alternative of unemployment. They managed to arrive at the hotel with no mishaps, so Severeno was told to put the jeep in the hotel garage and to pick Al up at seven tomorrow morning.

Al showered dressed and went down to the street level to find a taxi.

He hailed a brown colored 1940 Chevrolet taxi to go to Bob's house on the Prado. This relic had originally been used in La Paz but the hills became too much of an obstacle so it migrated to flatter terrain. The brown paint covered untold coats of Rustoleum and Bondo to hide the numerous dings in the fenders. This was another $0.50 ride.

Bob met Al at the door with a tall glass of Scotch on the rocks; he had seen Al get out of the taxi.

"Why don't we sit in the living room away from the kids?" Bob suggested. "Now, what do you think after one day on the site?"

Al started right off.

"We have to take a very close look at the core samples to see if we have been led astray through the lack of a well done geological study by the Engineers," he gave as the first priority for further study.

As he watched Bob's face, he realized he didn't want to get crosswise with Bob, as he was a very concerned and conscientious manager, so he tried to gently suggest that they had the following problems.

"If we suspect gross errors by the Engineer, we may have to bring in a well known geologist to back us up."

"Just off hand I would suggest that we have a supervisory problem. Jesus may be a good superintendent when he is above ground, but we need to have a top flight man underground on the TBM. I think we could work it so that we have one of each, by keeping Jesus on the above ground work and bringing in someone from the states with a known track record to bring Jesus up to speed for the TBM. This would be quite expensive but I believe it would be worth the cost."

He was trying to make these suggestions to Bob without making them requirements. Al was not making unfounded assumptions but rather educated analysis of the problem based on his experience.

Al told Bob that he thought they must revisit both George and Pedro.

"They are both probably excellent heavy equipment mechanics and operators, but we face a different situation here. We need a Master TBM Mechanic who knows TBMs inside and out to train and or support George, and we need three operators to actually become a living part of the machine. Again, I believe that we can bring a top flight machine operator in to teach the locals. These three men will be very expensive, but the rationale is that we can not afford a second line help in any of these spots. We must look at the cost of the machine vs. the relatively low outlay for a first class operator as a trainer."

Bob sat there looking relieved. He had someone on his side trying to get this project back on track.

"Thank you," Bob said, after a long draw on his scotch. "I sent a letter to my great white chief, the Regional Director of Operations for South America, requesting the very things you have just suggested. His very curt reply was to do as I am told and live with the budget that he had set up for this project. If I couldn't do that, then he would find someone who could. He is one cheap SOB."

Al pitched in with the thought that Bob's immediate leader was a misplaced bean counter from a cosmetics company.

"My orders are from the main office and that I am to be of assistance to you in every way possible, and damn the bean counters. If he doesn't like it, let him take it up with the main office."

"OK! When do we start the ball rolling?" he grinned. "Let's take a look at those core samples first thing in the morning. He can only fire me; it's against the law to draw and quarter me."

Their conference was broken up with the appearance of Agnes in the doorway. She suggested that they go out to a local restaurant for dinner and forget this nonsense.

"La Luna Bleu has some great seafood and wines, so let's go."

Al thought of his small, unsatisfying meal back at the hotel.

"Now I know who rules in this house. Agnes, you may not be very big, but I sure like the big club you carry. Let's go."

The three of them had a superb seafood diner with good wine and music. Al was informed that the mid week cocktail party was being held at the Suarez home at seven Wednesday evening, and that he was invited. As this was a mid week affair it would last only until eleven.

Al was beginning to think that this job might be one of the best ones he could ever have hoped for. But would he last? Time would tell.

Bob and Agnes dropped him at the hotel at ten so he could get a good night's sleep.

"See you at seven tomorrow so we can look at the core logs," Bob yelled as he drove away.

CHAPTER 15

Al woke up at an early hour to the sound of backfiring trucks and collectivos. They made so much racket that he found it impossible to sleep past six. He showered and shaved, put on his work clothes and caught the elevator as it lumbered down past his floor. He would have made better time walking down three levels to the ground floor. It was an alarming ride at this time of day as he still was not fully awake. The elevator lurched, screamed, groaned and occasionally stopped for a split second then continued its decent downward.

Al entered the dining room and was again greeted by the smiling waiter. This time he had a large pot of hot black coffee at the table before Al could sit down.

"I would like an omelet with mushrooms, cheese, and peppers with toast," Al said in English, in hopes that the waiter spoke enough English to get the order straight. He did, and it was very good.

Bob drove up to the hotel right on schedule to take Al to the drill core shed on the other side of town. Bob wanted to drive Al so that they could talk out the problems with the rock samples. Severeno would meet Al later at the job site.

"Let's go see what the drill cores have to show us," Bob said in a wide awake voice.

They drove across town to the warehouse where the cores were stored. The warehouse was an old rusted galvanized clad one story building with low tables two feet wide by forty feet long. There were three core boxes piled one on top of the other so that they had to lift each of them down to inspect them. The hinged covers when opened up showed five cores side by side and four feet long. The core boxes weighed about seventy-five pounds each. Al and Bob grunted and groaned picking each of those logged for the general area of the portal.

Bob noted, "The cores for the first 300 feet of tunnel must have come from another damned mountain. They're not even the same kind of rock that we have. Somebody really screwed up. It is obvious that the designers were marching to a different drumbeat. Not only that, but our estimator obviously never looked at the cores. Could that have been my leader? He's the one that came down here to bid the project. He had an estimator with him that came with him from his old company."

Al, looking a bit like a leopard sighting in on a lunch on legs, said, "This looks like a very good basis for claim in time and money that will cover all of your problems. Let's take photos to document this, just make sure we can see all the box labels as well as the cores in each box."

About three in the afternoon, they left to drive up to the job to start the program for getting the notice of claim going and to line out Jesus on how to retrieve the TBM.

They encountered Pierre Lamont when they arrived at the job site. Bob said, "We have major concerns with the core logs and what had been found when we inspected them."

Pierre did not seem to be pleased by the impromptu investigation, but said that he would contact his leaders in Montreal as soon as they gave him the official letter of Notice of Claim. He thought, "This could be a case of fraud on the part of the design firm."

"I don't think any of you know what you're talking about; you're trying to bull shit us. I'll personally deny any of your implied accusations," sneered Francois LaBatt, the Senor Construction Inspector on the project.

Both Bob and Al ignored his comments and left for their office.

"Just who the hell is that ass hole?" Al asked Bob when they had gained the privacy of Bob's office.

"He's the Construction Inspector on the site. He thinks he should be Resident Engineer. No one in Bolivia knows as much about everything as he does. He is doing his best to make enemies of the whole population," Bob stated with some animation. "Not only that, but he puts the make on every woman he gets near. That could be dangerous. Some of these guys pack guns."

They finished the claim letter and sent it on to Pierre.

"Let's call it a day and head for the barn," said Bob.

"Great. Just as soon as I get my report sent to my leader in San Francisco," Al answered.

Al's driver pulled up then. Bob waved them off, heading home to an evening of conversation that didn't focus on the project.

CHAPTER 16

At the hotel, Al cleaned up, and then went down to the bar for a before-dinner drink. He figured that he had earned it. He could see a light at the end of this tunnel and it wasn't the train coming down the track; they had a perfect basis for a sizeable claim.

Al bumped into George and Patricia Jordan as he walked into the hotel lobby. He started to speak to them but they seemed to be a bit up tight and shortly made excuses that they had to meet a driver to go to Santa Cruz. They left with him feeling a twinge of interest in who and what they were.

He recalled their statement he had overheard: "I know he's not my contact here."

Al went out to a local Italian restaurant for dinner where he ate ravioli and drank a class of Chianti. He returned to his room where he settled back with a mystery book, forgetting all about the Jordans.

Six in the morning arrived in a very inauspicious manner. No blare of trumpets, no sweet music and certainly no company in bed with him. He had the normal blurry eyes and a catch in his back. He figured that as long as he could put both feet on the floor and subsequently stand up, it would probably be a good day. Al performed his morning ablutions, dressed and wandered blindly to the questionably dependable elevator. It begrudgingly transported him to the ground floor and the restaurant door, where he was met by the smiling waiter with a pot of hot black coffee. Al had his fill of scrambled eggs and ham with toast.

Severeno drove up just as Al walked out the hotel door.

"Good morning, Severeno, how are you this morning? Al asked.

"Very well, thank you, Senor Provost. Are we going to the job office this morning?" asked Severeno.

"Yes, that we will, Severeno. I must go to work for a change."

The road had not widened any during the night and even seemed a bit narrower, especially on the sharp curves. Al marveled at the complete lack of safety signs and guardrails on the hairpin curves. He did learn that there were warning road signs all along the route. Severeno explained to him that washouts or roads blocked by rock slides were marked by intricate piles of rock. Their meaning was based upon the height, the type of rock pile and the number in a specific spot. Al had some trouble with this but felt that, as Severeno was driving, he could translate the meanings of the piles of rock.

He always felt better on the return trips because then they were on the uphill side of the road. Now they were on the drop off side of the road, looking straight down at times for some 400 to 500 feet. They started around a hairpin curve with Severeno sounding his horn, when a 2 ½ ton stake bed truck careened around the curve on their side of the road. The truck was piled about twelve feet high with coca leaf and five drunken campesinos hanging on the bales of coca for dear life. The driver and the other five of the occupants of the cab appeared as if they had been trying to drink all the chicha in Bolivia.

Al inadvertently yelled, "What the hell is wrong with that idiot?"

Severeno did not have time to answer as he swerved right to the extreme edge of the road and made a quick detour around the truck. All the while Al was staring down 500 feet at nothing any more substantial than air. Al was not at all certain that they would survive with one wheel hanging in space. He had to admit that Severeno was probably the best driver he had ever ridden with, or the luckiest.

After the near miss, all Severeno would say was, "I am sorry, senor."

The rest of the trip was uneventful.

Al was glad to step from the jeep. Spotting Bob waiting for him, Al quickly walked over.

"Hi!" said Bob, "Have a restful night?"

"Yes! But I damned near didn't live to get here. Are all the truck drivers crazy around here?" Then Al told him of their near miss.

Bob was sympathetic but not at all surprised at the encounter.

"Here, take this .45 Colt Auto. The next time you meet that idiot, just wave it in the windshield. I guarantee that will get his attention and he won't try to run you off the road again. Please don't shoot yourself with it."

Two days later, Al took Bob's advice and waved the .45 colt in the windshield when he saw the truck approaching. The effect was magical. The truck just seemed to jump sideways to get out of their way.

After that bit of advice they had gathered up Jesus Domingo, the general superintendent, and headed for the portal to plan the attack to salvage the TBM. They met Envero Aguilar, the union head, and the tunnel superintendent at the portal. They carried some drawings with them to lay out the work to be done. Envero painted the face on the rib of the tunnel about 50 feet behind the TBM and indicated the centerline of the new drift with paint so there would be little chance of getting off course.

"We plan to drive an access drift parallel to the main tunnel, 200 feet long, to get us past the TBM and the assumed broken ground," Bob directed both Domingo and Envero.

"Si, claro," said Envero. "It will be done."

Bob frowned. "I've heard enough "Si Claro" to last me a lifetime, and found that it really means 'yes, I understand, but I am going to do it my way.' So! This time this is the way it will be done. Claro?"

Envero smiled to himself. Senor Bob was trying to be the Big Boss, to impress that new man from California.

"We'll have to fabricate some timber square sets for the drift. Here are drawings of the square sets that we must make." Bob pointed out to Envero and Domingo. "How soon can you have, say, a half dozen of these ready? We'll get on the horn to the saw mill to order the timber we need for 50 sets for the drift. That should be enough for 200 feet of drift."

Al stood back, as this was Bob's show and he had to let them know that he was in charge and that he, Al, was there only to back him up if need be.

Domingo said, "We'll have two sets of ribs fabricated today and the other four by tomorrow afternoon. Will that be enough, Senor Adams?"

Bob answered Domingo, "That'll be fine. We'll start excavating the drift in the morning and as soon as we get more timber sets, (ribs), we'll go to three shifts to drive on past the TBM. We'll use the front end loader to muck out with, the same one we used for the machine cavern. You should get George Padilla to go over the drill jumbo to make sure it is ready to start work in the morning. I'll catch him just to be sure."

Bob and Al left the two men to go about reorganizing things by themselves. They didn't need either Bob or Al with them to bug the crew.

The crew set about drilling out the first round. They had finished by the end of the shift and were starting to load dynamite in the holes, when Al shouted, "What the hell are they tamping the powder with? Looks like drill steel. That's a wonderful way to blow the whole crew to hell and back."

The crew was indeed using drill steel for loading poles. They were loading dynamite with fused detonators. These detonators were prone to set off the dynamite with even a very small spark. Al let out a yell, "What is the matter with you people, don't you want to live another hour? You can very easily blow yourselves and anyone near you straight to hell using drill steel to tamp the dynamite. Get a life and learn how to work safe or clear out. Sorry, Bob, but I could not let that pass, I should not have yelled at them."

"I didn't see what they were doing or I would have yelled just as loud" Bob said.

They soon found that it was much preferable to use wooden loading poles. No spark that way and no explosion. This was pointed out to them in terms they could understand. They were a very lucky crew. The crew set off the round and there was a rather muffled explosion.

After the dust settled, about twenty minutes later, Bob and Al and Jesus walked back into the tunnel to the face. They found that only about half of the explosives had detonated. After digging around the muck pile, they found that the detonators had not been properly connected. The miners that were supposed to connect up the face were told that it was now their job to flush out the dynamite from the drill holes, re-load the holes with fresh dynamite and detonators, only this time they were to make certain that the explosives were correctly connected. Two hours later the blast was successfully set off. Such was the learning curve with untrained people.

Bob and Al left for the office to calm down.

"I would estimate that the drift should be back on the main tunnel line in about 25 days. It will probably take another 20 days to shut off the water inflow. That gives us time to get a crackerjack TBM superintendent as well as a proven TBM Master Mechanic and a first class TBM operator to teach the on site crew. Guess you need to start the ball rolling at headquarters. I will pave the way so you don't hit any speed bumps along the way," Al said to Bob.

Bob replied. "I'll contact the rib fabricator and pass the word to the main office as to the revised rescue plans as soon as we get to the office. Do you have any suggestions for people?"

"Yes! Glad you asked, as I just happen to know where we can find all of them, if they are willing to visit picturesque Bolivia. I'll wire San Francisco and have them bird dog those guys. We should hear from them by the first of next week," Al answered.

They stopped by Canadian Engineering Pty. Ltd (CE) to inform them as to what they planned to do. Pierre Lamont had no objections and indirectly gave his blessing.

A rather busy afternoon finally ended about six when they left to go back down to town.

With Severeno driving, they were winding their way down the mountain, when they were overtaken by a Canadian Engineering jeep roaring down the road like the Devil was on his tail. The driver started sounding his horn for Severeno to move out of his way. Severeno pulled over to the far right against the mountain while the CE jeep screamed by in a cloud of pebbles and dust and nearly lost it on the hairpin curve.

"That was Senor LaBatt. He drives like that all the time," said Severeno.

They were on the same hair pin curve where they were nearly run off the mountain by a truck earlier that morning.

"LaBatt could kill himself driving like that," Al thought.

That afternoon, after arriving in Cochabamba, Al had Severeno drive him to the office of Colonel Ovando Tajada, the military alcalde (mayor). Al entered the office and asked to see the alcalde. He asked the clerk to present the alcalde with some documents that were not to be shown to any one else. The clerk took him in rather sooner than Al had thought. Apparently the documents were the key.

"Good afternoon, Senor Provo, what can I do for you today?" asked the alcalde with a very toothy smile.

"Colonel Ovando Tajada, I desire a permit for a concealed weapon. I realize that this is an unusual request for a North American, but I would feel safer as well as more legal if I had a permit," smiled Al.

"Senor Provo, I would be honored to provide you with such a small item." As he said this, he called in his clerk. "Will you please make out a special Cartouche for Senor Provo for the carrying of a concealed weapon so that he may legally carry a weapon for hunting, fishing or for use in his line of work?"

Turning to Al, Tajada gave him another toothy smile.

"See, Senor Provo, how easy that was?"

"Colonel Tajada, I understand the hunting and fishing part, but what is that in his line of work?" queried Al.

"Ah yes. If someone steps in front of you with a gun and you shoot him, I will only have one piece of paper to fill out. But if someone steps out in front of you with a gun and shoots you, then I will be filling out papers for months. Just do me the favor of shooting first."

Twenty minutes later Al left the office with a permit that legalized the .45 auto that he had tucked under his belt. He had always been of the opinion that a .22 caliber could kill an assailant just as dead as could a .45 Colt. The difference though was the fact that the .22 caliber may not stop the bad guy while the .45 Colt will.

CHAPTER 17

Tonight was another free dinner at the Adams' home, a decided improvement over most of the restaurant meals Al could eat by himself. He had been told that there would be some Peace Corps Volunteers in town on R&R.

When Al got to Bob and Agnes's home, he was ushered into the foyer by a tall blond young lady who must have been all of twenty-one or two. He introduced himself and was told that he had the pleasure of meeting Sonya Sandal. Al was informed that she had a degree in nursing with a minor in languages. She was very trim and self confidant and well spoken. She spoke to Al in Castilian, then in mid sentence changed over to English. She took his arm and escorted him into the living room. She obviously was well educated and highly intelligent. Otherwise she would not have been as concerned that Al should meet every one in the room.

Al met George Johansen from Minnesota. He was a mid twenties-something, brown haired, rather stout young man. He stated that he had a degree in social studies with a major in languages.

He then met Elaine Clark of Colorado who had a BS in geology. She was a brown haired, slim muscular type that would probably have been more than happy to storm any and all of the Andes Mountains and never be short of breath. She was probably a skier and a mountain climber.

Peter Paine was the next young person that Al met. Al found out that he was from Georgia and studied music. He had his guitar with him for the evening's entertainment.

They sat at the dinner table, enjoying a great home-cooked meal, courtesy of Agnes's live-in cook, topped off with some very good brandy. This loosened everyone up so that the singing and story time began.

Sonya started by telling of her experience in the Beni in a mud hut shelter among a very primitive tribe that she was to try to help advance in the area of health and sanitation.

"I boarded a collectivo in Cochabamba. In case you have not yet had the dubious pleasure of riding 200 miles in a collectivo, let me tell you about them. They are normally old worn out truck frames with a tired bus body more or less attached to the frame with a few bolts. The head room is fine if you are only five feet tall. If you are any taller than that you bang your head on the roof every time you stand up. Standing up, however, can be a challenge as there isn't even any standing room. The collectivos are full of people, pigs, chickens and a few sheep. It seems that every campasina is carrying all her worldly goods on her back."

"This ride is both bone jarring and claustrophobic in that you are in such close contact with people who bathe only once a year, having the fear that they will wash away their protective layer of dirt. You do realize that these country people only take a bath when they accidentally fall into a stream. They all seem to have a symbiotic relationship with the biggest, strongest fleas in the free world. Of course the fleas are happy to have ample dirt in which to lay their eggs and to multiply. You can believe me when I say that they multiply. Those fleas are Olympic class jumpers."

"After enduring this we arrived in at our destination adjacent to the Rio Beni, and met Raul my guide to the Alta-agua tribe camp site. I was a bit dismayed when I saw the tired shaggy burros that were to be our transportation to the camp. I am bigger than they are, but Raul assured me that they were strong and dependable. I sure hoped he was right, especially when I asked him how long before we arrived at the camp. I was really upset when he told me it would be five days' journey on those poor burros. We camped out in the open at night, usually with a rain tarp for a roof to stay dry. The humidity was unbelievable. My clothes were drenched 24 hours a day. The bugs never gave up. We arrived at last at the camp of the Alta-agua."

"By this time I had lost all illusions as to being provided even decent accommodations. I was not disappointed. I was shown a mud hut with a palm leaf bed. The hut had a palm leaf door and a central fire pit. The two months I lived there, or to be more accurate, existed there, were very educational. I learned that when you have never had something like indoor plumbing, central air conditioning, and a comfortable bed, you don't miss them. I did not get to the point of not missing them. I did not, however, discard my clothing as had the people of this tribe. They mostly wore breech cloths and tattoos."

"I worked with those people trying to get them to live healthier lives, but learned that their primitive medicine worked very well for most of their problems. They have an amazing storehouse of plants that are curative of many illnesses. They don't really need us except to subvert their way of life."

"My time was up after two months and I joyfully mounted one of the burros and, five days later, after a hot shower and good food at the hotel, was grateful to climb aboard the collectivo to return to Cochabamba, fleas and all."

"That's my story," Sonya said, and reached for another beer.

George Johansen picked up another beer and decided to tell us a little of his experiences.

"I specialize in lost or forgotten languages. I was given the opportunity to come to Bolivia to find some of the lost tribes and to compile a dictionary of their language. To do this I spent several weeks in LaPaz getting information as to who and what peoples were out there in the jungles, or if any one knew what language they spoke or had any idea of where they could be contacted. I heard a lot of rumors but very few facts other than there is a tribe near the Rio Manore, or possibly on the Rio Isabella. These people were very shy and would have nothing to do with any other people in the area. I decided that my best bet was to go to Santa Cruz and on down the Rio Isabella where I could hire a local guide and a canoe to try to explore some of the streams feeding the main river. I traveled by local boat to Trinadad and found a hunter who would serve as a guide for me."

"Paulo seemed to be very interested in the money involved and claimed he could guide me safely down the river. I have since found that if you mention money everyone becomes an expert guide or whatever you want. Mention of money seems to trigger their mental responses as nothing else does."

"We traveled down river for several days before encountering some local fishermen who professed to know of a lost tribe that lived back in the jungle. After much hand waving and haggling over what we would pay them, they gave us vague directions."

"We followed their directions for a couple more days until we unexpectedly met a fisherman and his son. They were as surprised as we were, but did not run away. We gave them some fish we had caught and they invited us to follow them to their village. We probably lacked intelligence in this as they could have been inviting us to dinner as the main course. Fortunately they did not care for mock pig. I later learned that the head hunters lived farther out in the jungle."

"Paulo stated that he would stay with me as long as I needed him, for a price."

"One very interesting thing is that these people all have blue eyes. I have no idea how this could have come about, unless they were descended from European stock."

"We settled down in the village and hung out around the main campfire. I sat with them by the hour recording nearly every word they said and annotating my tapes and my notes with what was taking place. After the third day I was able to make a stumbling conversation with them. They treated us like members of the tribe and did all they could to make us feel welcome. I, like Sonya, did not go native and ditch my clothing, as they wore little or nothing. Overall I spent about three months with them until I could speak and think in their language as well as they did. I felt that I had accomplished my mission and now had a dictionary that provided a repository for their language. Interestingly enough, one could communicate with them with a vocabulary of less than one thousand words."

"Paulo and I loaded our belongings into the canoe and worried our way back to civilization. That's the end of my story," said George.

The rest of the evening was taken up by Peter Paine playing his guitar and starting an old fashioned sing along. They did not have a camp fire to gather around while they sang, but with a few more beers no one missed the dancing flames. These beers were 14% alcohol.

Elaine Clark told us about roaming the mountain sides doing a bit of geological exploring.

"I met a couple of campesinos last week up on the road above Mt Tunari near Jatun Rumi. They looked like they had been run through a meat grinder. Their faces and hands were all scratched and scabbed over. Their clothes were all torn and bloody, and they were limping along when I met them. I asked them in Quechua what had happened to them. After a rather long, hesitant, and obviously embarrassed pause they told me that they had found what we would call road kill on the side of the mountain and carried it up to an adobe house near the top of the mountain. The adobe was about 12 by 16 feet, with a door and no windows, but it did have a roof. They placed the road kill near the door of the adobe with a rope firmly tied so it could rapidly be pulled back into the casa. They then sat in the adobe all day and about half the next day before a giant Andean Condor spotted the road kill and dropped in for a meal. The ingenious duo pulled the rope and the rancid carcass into the adobe. The Condor, being hungry, followed on into the casa. Our intrepid trappers then closed the door from the inside intending to grab the Condor, tie him up and carry him back to civilization to sell to a zoo. It did not take long for them to realize their mistake. A Condor with a twelve foot wingspan and two inch talons plus a five inch beak can do a major amount of damage in a very short time. The mighty hunters admitted that what was probably only a matter of several minutes seemed like an eternity before they could get the door open and scramble out of the adobe, and away from their intended prey. They declared that they were not about to trap any more Condors. They watched the Condor strut out into the open and fly away, no worse for the troubles they had given him."

Elaine was still laughing even after telling her story. We admitted that it was a story about misplaced intelligence.

The group for some reason got onto the subject of chicha. Al learned that it is made of corn. It is the original corn licker, only with a twist. The campesinos grind the kernels of corn, mix the meal and leave it outside the adobe during the night to freeze. The next day after it thaws out they crush it even more by walking around in the meal with their bare feet. They go through the same process for several days. They then sit around a small fire with an inverted cone pot propped up in the embers. They take a mouthful of the meal and chew it. This mixes with the enzymes in their mouths and, when spit into the cone and heated, it starts fermenting. By the next day it has an alcohol content of around 14%. This is strong enough to send the average Cholo into orbit after several quarts have been consumed. They then remain in that condition for several days.

The party broke up soon after because most of them had to go to work early in the morning.

"Don't forget the cocktail party at the Quirogas on Saturday night the 1st," admonished Agnes as we were leaving. "Be ready to stay around for the evening."

CHAPTER 18

"Another day on the front lines," Al quipped as he walked out the door to Severeno and the waiting Jeep. After all he had just finished a good breakfast and was ready for about anything.

"Good morning, Severeno. Did you have a good evening?" Al asked, hoping that he had not been listening to the radio reports on the Carrera Pan Americano (Pan American Road Race). It seems as though every time he did he started to drive like he was one of the lead drivers in the race. Severeno did get quite excited about the road race from Buenos Aires to Panama.

"Yes!" Severeno answered. "Do you wish to go to the job again this morning?"

"I'm in no great hurry. Just drive slowly," Al said.

They had just cleared the first switchback when Severeno had to stand on the brakes to avoid a large boulder in the middle of the road. It was very fortunate for both of them that there was some space between the boulder and the vertical sidewall of the road cut, and that they were moving quite slowly. The brake pedal went all the way to the floor with no pressure. The brakes were inoperable. They scraped the sidewall and came to a grinding stop. Severeno jumped out of the jeep and raised the hood. He made some loud remarks in Quechua, that when translated told Al that the brakes were out of fluid. He soon found that it had drained out of the brake hose near the left front wheel. Someone had punched a hole in it. They got back into the Jeep and drove very slowly using the gears to slow the Jeep and the emergency brake to bring it to a stop at the office. The hose was replaced at the workshop and brake fluid was added so they could return safely to town in the afternoon.

"Bob, I am beginning to get the feeling that someone around here does not like me. Am I being paranoid?" asked Al.

They arrived at the job just as the first round was shot in the access drift. The delays sounded a little ragged. The explosions were not evenly spaced. Al wondered why, and decided to find out what caused the problem. The powder smoke billowed out of the vent line in an orange cloud. One could smell nitro-glycerin from the dynamite.

He went into the office to a meeting with Bob, Domingo and Alberto, going over the alignment for the side-drift that would by-pass the TBM. They were discussing the problem of shooting clean ribs as it is nearly impossible to acquire uniformly spaced delays for detonating the dynamite. That caused problems in breaking out the rock in a uniform pattern. The next problem was that the dynamite was much higher velocity than they needed so that they would not get the blasted rock in the size that they wanted

It was 78% nitro glycerin rather than the 50% that they had ordered. They had to compensate for this in their blasting pattern so that they did not shatter the rock around the TBM. The crew was conscientiously using wooden loading poles to tamp the dynamite.

Domingo said that the third and forth timber rib fabrications were progressing and they should be ready by morning.

"We have hopes of obtaining a continual advance of three four-foot rounds per day in the by-pass tunnel, after we start three shifts. We should hole through ahead of the TBM in about seven weeks. This is a little slower that I had hoped for, but we must remember where we are," Al said. "We can pick up some time if the miners can start pulling six foot rounds on each shift. That would possibly get us to the TBM in four weeks."

"The saw mill called us to say that they could increase their delivery to get all the timber for ribs that were needed within two weeks."

They went into the tunnel to see how the last shot pulled the rock and to see the crew setting the first timber rib. Al was moderately pleased at their progress.

Bob, Alberto and Al met with Pierre Lamont and Ian MacDonald of Canadian Engineers Pty Ltd to review their plans and to reiterate the need of their making some arrangements for a major changed conditions claim.

"Do you want us to go on force account for the tunnels to rescue the TBM?" Bob asked. "If you don't want to do that, then we'll have to shut down all operations until we receive your written instructions as to what actions you (CE) want us to perform."

Pierre said, " I received directions from the owner that this project will not be shut down and that I'm to issue a directive to BOSCO to continue work under force account, at least until we can come to some mutual agreement on the overall costs."

"I presume that one of you will be signing off each shift as we advance." said Bob.

"Actually it will be Francois LaBatt as Senor Construction Inspector who will tabulate the work force and the equipment used so that your people can sign off each day. You and I can then get together on a daily basis to agree or disagree," remarked Pierre. "Well, I guess that winds this up for today, right?"

"Let's call it a day," said Bob.

They went back to their offices to rehash their meeting with Pierre and Ian. It was about lunch time, so they paraded to the mess hall. There were two dining areas, one for the workers and one for the supervisory and engineering staff. The management group had their own table out of the way of the rest of the people. Al was told that he could get breakfast there rather than in the restaurant, if he were to crawl out of bed early enough. That sounded like it might be worthwhile. Al decided he would try it out to see what nauseous food they would serve.

At about two that afternoon, they heard a lot of noise near the compressor house, and looked out to see a major confrontation taking place between Domingo and LaBatt. By the time they arrived at the battleground they found that a number of the miners had grabbed Domingo to prevent him laying it on LaBatt. LaBatt, in the meanwhile, was held back by some of the other miners. His loud voice could be heard for some distance. He was calling Domingo and all the miners everything he could think of in both French and Spanish. He railed at the ancestry and siblings of all the miners as well as Domingo. Al was not at all sure that some of the miners were not going to take him to task for all of his very rude and vulgar descriptions of their parentage. LaBatt did not understand that in this part of the world a person can disappear without trace for the grand sum of $8.00. LaBatt was doing his utmost to make enemies. In general, things like this did not go unavenged among the miners.

They managed to calm the miners down and separate them from LaBatt. They got Domingo to take a few days off with pay to salvage his self respect.

They decided that they had had enough for the day and left to go to town. They were all still pretty uptight about the potential ramifications of this afternoon's conflict. A CE Jeep came roaring down the road, skidding around the hairpin curves, scattering dirt and gravel in all directions. LaBatt went careening past the men again.

Al thought to himself, "Maybe he does have the Devil on his tail after all."

DICK ROBERTS

Al went to the hotel, showered and dressed for dinner at a local restaurant. He had several stiff Scotch on the rocks to calm him down after this past day. He went back to the hotel to get a good night's rest.

Al thought," This was going to be a walk in the park, but seems like there is always something screwing up the peace and quiet. Wonder what will be next?"

CHAPTER 19

The next morning saw him up and ready to go as soon as Severeno drove up. He had decided to try breakfast at the camp mess hall.

"How are the brakes this morning?"Al asked.

Severeno said," I checked them and I also found the S.O.B. that punctured the brake hose. After threatening to cut off his balls and shoving the knife up between his legs he would not stop talking. He told me that some foreigner paid him $10.00 to do it as a joke on you. He didn't know who the person was nor could he give me a good description."

"At least we know it wasn't the fault of our mechanics," said Al.

His appetite took leave of him on the trip up the grade. They looked up the hill to the next hairpin curve and watched as a collectivo careened around the curve and fly off the side of the mountain like a giant bird. It bounced a half a dozen times before crashing in the bottom of the canyon 500 feet below. Every bounce split the shell open a bit more and bodies flew out like watermelon seeds. Bodies of the unfortunate occupants were strewn all the way to the canyon floor. There was nothing that either Severeno or Al could do. They could not get down to the bodies as the side wall was nearly vertical. They drove on to camp and called the local police.

"There's always something around here. Never a dull moment," said Al, telling Bob of the latest developments.

Al went to the tunnel and saw that they had advanced about eight feet total. The newly milled timber for the timber ribs was beginning to arrive on site. The miners were learning how to work with the delays and the high velocity dynamite. There had been no more outbursts from LaBatt; however the air was thick with animosity toward him. Everyone seemed to be trying to ignore LaBatt, hoping that he would blow away in the wind or drive off the side of the mountain.

Bob and Al talked to Pierre about sending LaBatt back to Canada before anything drastic happened.

He said, "I will think about it and let you know. If I did send LaBatt home, it would be after his replacement arrived on site. This could take up to a month."

"In the meantime you might suggest to LaBatt that he drive a bit more cautiously or you may not have to worry about an airline ticket for him. There won't be enough left of him to send home," Al told him of the wild driving habits of LaBatt.

Pierre talked to LaBatt about his confrontation with Domingo and his wild driving, suggesting the possibility of sending LaBatt back to Canada. LaBatt erupted like a small Krakatau. He was incensed that anyone would even consider this move.

"I cannot go back to Canada; too many people are waiting for me there, It has to be that Provo who put Pierre up to this. I will have to take care of that problem," he muttered to himself as he walked stiffly out of Pierre's office.

Needless to say after that previous day's happenings, Al was not very cordial to anyone. The project could not afford a major confrontation or an unexplained accident.

The rest of the day passed rather calmly except for the police wanting a statement on the accident Al and Severeno had witnessed earlier in the day.

He found Severeno and they left in the jeep to return to town. This trip was uneventful, with no careening truck loads of coca leaf or any crazy jeep drivers. Severeno dropped Al off at the hotel where he was able to cleanup for the evening meal.

Al decided to visit the Tunari brewery for a quiet dinner on the terrace overlooking Cochabamba. He found another worn out taxi that still had enough get up and go to make it up the hill to the brewery. Al arranged for the taxi to come back and pick him up in about three hours. He figured that he could dispose of enough Bolivian beer by then that he would not be upset about the taxi drive back to town. Bolivian beer was a 14% beverage, and at 8500 foot altitude does pack a wallop.

Al had some fresh frozen camarons (shrimp) recently flown in from Chile. The camarons were liberally coated with coconut, and sautéed to a turn. Wine had been drizzled over them for an added flavoring. He was also served baby carrots with wine sauce. He passed on the salad but did partake of the conch chowder. The conchs were imported from Chile and were a favorite sea food dish in Cochabamba. The German chocolate cake was out of this world. He topped all of this off with a brandy and a cup of very good black coffee. The coffee was grown in the eastern foothills near

Via Tunari. The beans were roasted and sent up the mountain before they were dried out, leaving them with a very distinctive flavor.

The taxi arrived and Al returned to the hotel at a reasonable hour. Lacking anything worthwhile to occupy him, he drifted into the hotel bar and ordered a scotch on the rocks to help relax. After a few glasses of double Scotch on the rocks, he wandered over to the elevator. He had to listen to its squeaks and groans as it came down to the ground floor. The elevator labored up to the third floor as though it might not make another assent. He hurriedly went to his room just to get away from that decrepit piece of machinery.

CHAPTER 20

The elevator was waiting for him the next morning as he went down to meet Severeno and the jeep.

They were almost to the cumbre (pass) when a herd of llama crossed the road in front of them. At the same instant, a second herd crossed from the other side of the road. Al was spellbound watching them cut through one another without so much as a by your leave. One herd had red yarn at the top of each ear of the llama, while the other herd had brown colored yarn at the top of each ear of the llama. Some of the llama had lost the top half of their ears because they had been frozen and fallen off. The variations of black, brown and white were intriguing. Their shaggy wool hung in clumps on their shoulders and bellies. They had not yet been shorn of their wool this year.

They never even turned their heads to look at one another. They walked with their long necks stretched vertically and their heads held high in a haughty posture that suggested that they knew they were the most important thing in the Andes. In a way they were: they have provided transportation, wool and meat to the Cholas for several thousand years.

The herders whistled and squeaked strange noises that the llama all seemed to understand.

Al did learn that llama in the mountains generally had communal areas for their excrement. These areas were devoid of all vegetation as the excrement was very acid. One story was that some Gringos figured that this would make excellent fertilizer for their gardens. This proved to be a major mistake as the garden plants were burned out by the very acid llama manure.

The herds left the road and continued on toward their individual destinations high up in the mountains.

Severeno and Al continued on to the job, where Al immediately went to the mess hall for breakfast. Bob, Domingo, and Jesus were already there, as were most of the rest of the staff. Al sat down at the table with them.

"The crew has advanced the tunnel heading a total of eight feet. They're getting pretty well lined out now," Domingo noted. "If they keep this advance every day, we should be back in front of the TBM within the month. We're getting delivery on the timber for the ribs, so we'll be OK."

"Is the crew getting any of the rock off the trailing floor? That and the damage repair must be completed before we can ever move the TBM. We may have to re-manufacture some of the trailing floor structure before moving on," Bob reminded Domingo and Jesus.

They were both agreed that the work had to be done as soon as possible.

Bob and Al went to the office. Bob had a message from his leader complaining about his going over his head to get approval for experienced help but did say the people he had requested would be arriving in about two weeks. They were to be temporary as trainers for the people on site. Bob would be the judge of when the training was completed.

"Bob, it looks like you are between a rock and a hard place. You had to add the temporary training bit. If your boss gives you any grief, let me know and I'll see that he gets off your back and stays off," Al said.

Bob did not know that Al had wired John Christman telling him that while bad rock did provide problems on the project, the micro-managing by the South American Manager was even more detrimental to progress of the work. Bob would have to be backed by the South American Manager, not called on the carpet every time that he wired home for special help or equipment.

"The training bit may save some hurt feelings with Domingo and Jesus, for whatever that is worth," Al added.

"The experienced boring machine operators, the drivers, are of utmost importance. It is penny wise and dollar foolish to put a $5.00 a day machine operator on a $6,000,000 machine. The length of training time depends on the local operators," Al continued. "Let's go see the headings to get a better feel for the work taking place."

They went into the tunnel and nosed around the drift; however Al became very uneasy as he noted that the usual timbering was missing behind the rib supports. Rocks were dribbling down from the crown until suddenly all hell broke loose. About 20 feet of tunnel crown collapsed behind them. The fallout extended up into the crown about 15 feet and about 20 feet long. The party found themselves in a room some 30 feet long. This section of tunnel seemed to be stable. Looking back at the rock pile behind them Al could only guess that someone in their infinite wisdom had decided that since the timber lagging was in short supply, the only reasonable alternative was to rob lagging from the previously supported tunnel. They were trapped like rats in a trap.

Al growled, "It is a damned good thing we got through that section of tunnel, Now all we have to do is get out of here, I hope that someone out there has the sense to start re-timbering the crown, at least enough so that we can crawl out."

They started carefully removing fallen rock near the crown of the tunnel They started building a crib to support the loose rock above. This was a very slow and tedious procedure as they did not want to disturb more rock above them. They could hear the miners doing the same thing from the portal end of the rock fall.

The re-timbering took about two hours until there was a big enough crawl space for the men to exit the trap. They crawled out and thanked their lucky stars that they were still alive. As they left for the office they could hear Domingo shouting some very unkind things to the miners in Quechua. To Al's minimal ability in Quechua, the shouting indicated Domingo's ire at nearly being killed by someone's stupidity. There was an implied threat that if it ever happened again, there would be retribution in the form of the perpetrator finding himself learning to fly as he hurtled over the side of the mountain.

The rest of the day was spent reviewing the draft for the changed conditions claim that Will Barret and Alberto Lopez were working on. They were correlating all the available data from the bid documents and setting up comparisons with the actual cores stored in town and the conditions that had been encountered to date.

Al suggested that they go ahead with what they were doing, but wait until the TBM was once again advancing, before considering completing the claim and submitting it. The entire length of the tunnel could turn out to be one great big changed condition.

"We don't want to pass up this opportunity to really cover our respective asses," Al smilingly finished.

They finally called it a day and headed for town.

Al decided that he needed a little quiet time so he went to an old John Wayne movie in black and white. It was in English with Spanish sub-titles. Al was not at all certain that the sub-titles in Spanish were fitting the dialogue in English, because there were peels of laughter and clapping of hands at the wrong times. One of these was when he and his fighter squadron were airborne and he got on the radio to tell the other pilots to put on their oxygen masks because they were about to climb to 10,000 feet. Many of the movie goers lived above 10,000 feet and had never seen an oxygen mask.

Another story often repeated by the locals was about a visiting group of dignitaries donning oxygen masks while touring the Altiplano at 13,500 feet.

Al enjoyed the fact that the film was a bit slow in starting, causing all the movie goers to stamp their feet on the wood floor. That really got the projectionist's attention.

After the movie, Al had dinner at the hotel and called it a night.

CHAPTER 21

Al was beginning to settle in to the antics of his driver, so closed his eyes for what he expected to be an uneventful ride up the mountain. Suddenly, he sensed electricity in the air, a drastic change in Severeno's driving, as they rounded the curve just below the cumbre.

Two men armed with AK 47's jumped in front of the jeep and fired several shots. One shot went through the driver's window and grazed Severeno's shoulder. Al's reflexes saved him from catching a bullet meant for him. The instant that the armed men stepped in front of the Jeep, Al threw open the passenger door and rolled out onto the ground putting the Jeep between him and the gunmen. As he was in mid flight, he drew the .45 colt from his belt and thumbed off the safety. When he hit the ground, he drew down on the nearest attacker and fired one head shot. He then swiveled his hand, lining up the second man in his sights, but moved the muzzle enough so that he only wounded the man. The second man fell to the ground moaning and convulsing in pain. Al stood, walked to both men, making certain that the first one was dead and that the second could not reach his AK 47. He stooped over the assailant to ask him what this had been all about.

"You seem to have made a grave mistake, Senor. I want to know who told you to do this. Please answer me so I won't have to hurt you more."

The would-be assassin spit at Al.

He looked at the shooter in disgust, and snapped at him that he was not going to screw around with him. He wanted answers now. If the right answers did not come in the next several minutes, if no answers were immediately provided, then he would use the very large sharp knife he was holding in his right hand to cut off his manhood, right down to its roots. Al approached the man and spread his legs to get a clear view of the man's crotch.

This maneuver resulted in the shooter's clutching his crotch in defense.

"You know, I don't think that I will use the knife. That would be very bloody, and some of your blood might splash on me. I'll tell you what I am going to do. I'm going to shoot off your manhood with my .45 Colt."

Al thumbed off the safety and fired a shot just missing the man's crotch. "Oops! I missed, have to try again. I'll try to hold steadier this time."

Al swung the pistol back so that it pointed at the assailant's crotch. This brought much different reaction as the man cried out. "It was the Cuban, Senor Ortega, who hired us to do this. He said that you were the one that turned in Che Gueverea to the US Special Forces to give him to the Bolivian Army. He said that you were the contact man for Che here in Bolivia. You were to be shot, and then taken to Ortega's camp in the Jungas below Pampa Tambo. He was going to make an example of what he does to traitors. Please don't kill me. I am just a poor cholo who was given $20 to do this."

Al turned to Severeno to see how badly he had been hit.

"I'm sorry it took me a few minutes more than I thought, but I had to make sure what was happening before he died. It looks like you were very lucky, only a flesh wound. I had no idea anything like this would happen."

A shadow moved across the group of men on the road. Al looked up toward the summit and saw an Andean Condor gliding on the thermals, its head swiveling at the end of its long neck looking for food. Seeing nothing worthwhile, it continued on its flight.

"Damn, Severeno. I feel like someone just flew over my grave. That's a big bird up there. If only he could talk, what tales he could probably tell."

Al kept his eyes on the bird until it soared out of sight, then sighed heavily and pulled himself back into the present.

"Damn it!" he said more to himself than his driver. "That was three years ago that I was sent down here to ferret out Che so that the SF could corner him. I'm very glad that my instructor at Langley was so difficult to please. He said one day his pushing me to such a high level of response and reflexes would save my life, but that was in 1954 after I sobered up and before I started working as a miner, as a cover," mused Al.

"Look, he's getting away," cried Severeno.

"That's OK. He'll lead us back to Ortega, and I'll follow him."

"No, Senor. We will follow him, as my orders are to protect you. I am under orders from the Chief Perez. I am a police officer doing undercover work," confessed Severeno.

"OK then. Do you happen to have a radio in your pack so that you can tell chief Perez that there's a body up here and that we're going after the rest of the gang?" asked Al.

They waited until they heard the wounded man leave in the jeep that he had hidden around the corner. They then followed him in the distance. They drove back to Cochabamba, then out the road to Punata, then up the cumbre and down to the Colomi turnoff. Their quarry had taken the old road down the mountain to Pampa Tambo past the power house and on down to a place that Al knew. They stopped the Jeep and both of them walked silently through the jungle growth to peer down on the camp.

Al had his .45 Colt as well as one of the AK 47s, and Severeno had the other AK 47. They watched as their attacker went into the camp and reported to the one they thought was Ortega. A lot of gesturing went on and angry voices came up to them through the underbrush. Ortega then turned to the man, pointed a pistol at him, and shot him in the chest.

"Let that be a lesson to the rest of you. I do not tolerate failure to carry out my orders," Ortega shouted at the remaining three men.

Al shouted at Ortega telling him to drop his gun and to lie flat on the ground. Ortega replied as Al thought he would, with a hail of bullets. Al and Severeno both fired at the group, dropping three of assailants. It was a very short gun fight, with three of the assassination squad now dead. The fourth man, presumably Ortega, had slipped out of the field of fire and was scampering through the jungle underbrush. Al followed closely behind him, keeping out of Ortega's line of sight.

This could develop into a cat and mouse game that Al knew all too well. He remembered playing this kind of deadly game with the Viet Cong in Vietnam while on a covert operation to rescue American POW's being held in a jungle compound in 1964. He had been tapped for the mission by the Special Forces Delta Unit, he recalled. He remembered that every time he heard a bird fly by or a small animal moved through the jungle, he had developed a strong case of runny bowels.

It was no different here in Bolivia. The prey was very dangerous, Al thought, and he didn't have the luxury of misjudging any of him.

Al heard Ortega about 50 feet ahead of him. Al dropped to the ground and crawled quietly through the brush, never making a sound or causing the brush to move and give him away. He suddenly started worrying that the sound of his beating heart would give his location away. He concentrated on reducing his reaction to fear and managed to get his heart beat lowered, at least the noise, if not the rate. Al slowly pushed aside a small plant and there sat Ortega sighting over the barrel of his AK 47.

Unfortunately for Ortega, he had misjudged Al and was aiming about 30 degrees away from Al's approach line. Al slowly slid his trigger finger over the trigger of the AK 47 that he was carrying, sighted down the barrel at Ortega and called softly for Ortega to drop his weapon. Ortega started to swing toward the sound of Al's voice, but never made it. Al squeezed the trigger, ending the pursuit instantly.

Al sat and thought about what had just taken place. He had been through this sort of thing a number of times but still did not feel good about killing a man, no matter that the man deserved it or if it had been ordered by his commanding officer. There had been a few times like today, when it was either him or the other guy.

"Severeno, why don't you try your radio again to let the Chief know where the rest of this group of failed assassins is? By the way, feel free to take all of the honors for shooting them while defending me," Al suggested.

Severeno smiled and put out his hand to congratulate Al on his quick reflexes and his marksmanship.

After Severeno notified Chief Perez and was told the police would be there in about an hour, he and Al left as though nothing had happened. They drove back to the job, getting there at noon. Al told Bob about being attacked and that Severeno had protected him. Bob did not buy that version but let it go without asking any more questions.

Bob had begun to wonder just what Al was really all about. "Here is a guy that is a top construction man, yet when the chips were down he could take out an attacker as though it were second nature to him. He had highly tuned reflexes that would make one hope that he was on their side when things got rough."

Bob shook his head, as though to clear his thoughts. Turning to Al, he decided the best approach was to be as matter of fact as possible.

"We're making some good progress now. The tunnel crews have once more advanced the heading twelve feet. This gives us a total to date of forty feet of access tunnel excavated. That's quite good, considering the rock that the tunnel was being driven in. The claim paperwork seemed to be coming along a bit better than anticipated."

Both men stood and looked at each other. It was evident that each was reading the other quite well. An unspoken agreement seemed to float in the air that they would not discuss further the morning's happenings.

Al left the job in the early evening with Severeno driving him to town.

CHAPTER 22

His evening was again spent walking around the city and doing a bit of exploring into the heart of the concha (open air market). He found that it was ill advised to walk there looking at anything other than where one was placing his feet. It seemed that a large share of the garbage of Cochabamba resided on the grounds of the concha. The odor was quite pungent. The open air market place covered a very large block with many small stores surrounding the square.

Al found that he could buy just about anything he wanted in the concha. It was no secret that one could buy canned hams courtesy of the Catholic Relief Society, or canned butter and any number of US canned goods as well as nylon hose, rubber boots, shoes and, sunglasses straight from Europe. If one were daring, he could even buy Argentine whiskey or genuine Scotch. Let the buyer beware, thought Al, as his eyes took in stall after stall of goods. Most of the bottles of alcohol had the bottoms drilled, the good stuff drained out and rot-gut whiskey poured back in. All of these goodies were courtesy of the local smugglers union.

On the far side of the square was a large ornate building that had been built in the 1950's to be the main railroad station on the line from LaPaz to Santa Cruz. The reality was that the railroad existed from LaPaz through Cochabamba on to Aiquile where it suddenly stopped. It had advanced at the leisurely pace of about a mile per year since then. The mountainous terrain made track building and grades very difficult.

Al saw a large - by Bolivian standards - gathering of cholos crowded around a rather tall, impressive individual wearing the usual knitted hat over his jet black shoulder length hair. The hat was knitted with all sorts of designs. He had a multi colored poncho thrown over his left shoulder, partly covering his home spun white shirt and trousers. The trousers were held up by a very colorful woven belt. His deep black eyes took in everyone in the crowd. He held a six foot long walking staff in his right hand. It had a gold rope wound around the staff with a silver and gold condor mounted at the very top.

It was impossible to tell which was the most startling, the silver and gold condor or the cholo dignitary from the west side of the Andes in Peru. Al later learned that the appearance of visitors from the other side of the Andes was not at all unusual. No one was able to say why these emissaries traveled from one side to the other and along the length of the Andes. It was possible that the cholos knew but weren't telling the gringos.

The next day Al told Bob of his walk through the concha. Bob started to laugh and said, "Last Saturday I went to the concha with Agnes. She seemed to think that she just had to go there. We walked around, high stepping over whatever covered the ground, when Agnes saw a poncho that she liked. She asked the Indian woman how much it cost. She was told that it was priced at $30.00 US. Agnes, being wise to negotiating, offered $10.00 US. The woman said no. Agnes started to walk off when the woman offered it for $25.00 US. Agnes again said no, but she would give $12.00. The sales woman started talking to her friend in Quechua. They decided that $15.00 was as low as she could go. Little did she realize that the dumb gringo husband - me," Bob laughed, "understood her, and was telling his wife in English what the conversation was all about. Agnes then offered $15.00 and said that was all she would pay, take it or leave it. The Indian sales woman took the ready cash, still shaking her head trying to figure out just how she had been beat down to her base price."

Al was becoming aware of the weather differences, between California and Bolivia. The weather changed very little as the job was located about eighteen degrees off the equator. He'd been told, also, that there was actually little seasonal change, that the mountains just become shrouded with snow in mid winter. Fortunately, the tunnel was just below the snow line.

So he was not surprised when Severeno met him at the door of the hotel with the word that there would reportedly be ice that night up on the mountain, but it would thaw by mid morning.

At the job site that day, Bob reported that they were still doing well and advanced another twelve feet for the three shifts. This gave the tunnel a total to date of sixty-six feet excavated. The rock apparently was more massive and did not tend to fall out of the roof as it had before.

CHAPTER 23

That Saturday, when Al checked on the progress at the site, he found the rock was improving, and the total advance for the past 24 hours was twelve feet. This gave a total to date of seventy-eight feet of access tunnel excavated. He roamed around in the tunnel to see how the crew was doing, then went back to the office to see Bob.

"Looks like things are all on course," said Al.

"We seem to be moving in the right direction with this thing. Thanks for the shoulder to lean on," replied Bob.

That about finished the morning, so Al decided to go back to town.

"Come on by about one and we will grab a bite before the big parade Saturday afternoon," Bob reminded him. "Oh! Don't forget the party tonight at the Quirogas."

Al went to the hotel and cleaned up before meeting Bob and Agnes and family at a little sidewalk café on the Prado that would afford a curbside seat for the parade. They ordered sultanas and beer and coke for the kids.

This parade apparently was an annual event celebrating the beginning of autumn and the harvesting season. The campesinos came down out of the mountains to celebrate in the villages and in the city.

"Look over there. I can see the parade starting at the end of the Prado near the bridge," said Rita, the Adam's number one daughter. "Can't you hear the drums and pan flutes?"

Indeed, they could hear the commotion at the other end of the street. There were a group of cholos bunching up behind some people beating on drums, blowing on the pan pipe flutes and playing charangos (one quarter sized guitar probably brought to Bolivia by the Spanish). Al soon realized that Andean music of this kind played on both radio stations and never shut down. It did get to be a little tiring after a few days. A North American used to jazz can only handle so much drumming, flute playing and an untold number of charangos. The songs in both Quechua and Aymara all seemed to be to the same music and did get somewhat repetitious.

The dark complexioned women were dressed in flowing dresses that covered several layers of dresses. Their bodices were mostly white cotton, billowing at the shoulders and tied at the waist by a woven alpaca belt. The dresses were like Joseph's many-colored coat, however only in brown, red, blue, yellow and green, the only colors named in the Quechua language. They all had ponchos in the same varied colors. The hats were of different styles, depending upon their origins. A round brown bowler indicated that they were from the Altiplano while a white stovepipe with black ribbon was a Cochabamba style. Most of the women were shod in black patent leather shoes or zapatos made of discarded rubber tires.

The men, with the same round faces and short squat barrel-chested bodies, wore woven alpaca trousers, usually white, tied at the waist by a woven alpaca belt. Their shirts were frequently multi-colored, covered by the typical colored poncho of brown, red, yellow, or green. Some of them wore hand knit sweaters of brown or grey with many different symbols, such as stair steps to heaven, condors, or llamas, woven into the alpaca wool.

Most of the men wore zapotos of reclaimed rubber tires. The men all wore knitted form fitting hats that extended down over the ears. These were highly decorated with Inca symbols embedded in the brown or grey alpaca wool. All of their outer garments were of alpaca as that wool was exceptionally warm and reasonably water resistant. The yarn was hand spun, and when knitted into a sweater invariably had a variety of small sticks or grass interwoven in the fabric.

The rather noisy parade passed the café where Al and Bob and family were sitting. The clamor of drums, flutes and charangos were accompanied by a chorus of singers, with songs in the Quechua and Aymara languages as they dance in the street. It seemed that their favorite songs were WaWa-Wat'a and Naranjita (the first being Little Baby and the second being Little Orange) in Quechua.

The parade lasted for several hours until the music was embedded in their minds. They had about exhausted their capacity for beer and the young ones had exhausted their patience as well as that of the parents, so it was decided to call it a day, at least until this evening.

Al walked back to the Adams' abode where he and Bob decided to partake of a Scotch on the rocks.

"You met the Colonel the other day, didn't you?" Bob asked. "Well, he has a rather interesting history. I was told the other day that he has more lives than a cat. One of the stories is that he was in his bed alone (apparently a first for him) when he had to get up in the middle of the night to go to the bathroom. While he was in the bathroom, someone threw a bomb through the window and it rolled under his bed where it exploded rather violently, tearing up most of the room and furniture. The Colonel was quite shaken by this attempt to rid the republic of his services. No one was ever found or at least publicly accused of this foul deed."

"Talking about an interesting history and having nine lives, you seem to be gaining on the Colonel," Bob muttered quietly.

Al politely ignored Bob's remark.

Agnes suggested that they meet at the hotel at seven to go on to the cocktail party. That sounded like a good plan so Al left for the hotel via taxi.

CHAPTER 24

After dressing for the party, Al had a light dinner to tide him through the evening, and then wandered out to the street to meet Bob and Agnes.

They drove to the Quirogas on a rather nice, well kept, side street. They lived in a very nice large Victorian home that dated back to the early 1900's. It was a red brick two story home on a large corner lot completely enclosed by an eight foot high brick wall with barbed wire and broken glass embedded in the top. A large swing gate opened after Al and Bob had identified themselves. The house was sited on about an acre of landscaped ground, all inside the wall.

The front door was an eight foot wide double door of heavy oak with wrought iron fixtures. Al had to stop and gape as they entered a foyer that made movie sets look pale. The living room had to be at least forty feet wide by fifty feet long with cathedral ceiling and second floor balconies overlooking the area. About forty couples were gathered near the bar, with only a few standing like wall flowers in odd corners.

Bob introduced Al to the host and hostess, Ambassador Juan Quiroga and his lovely wife Constantia.

"This is the Ambassador from Chile, Al. They live in Cochabamba as they have problems with the high altitude in LaPaz. He is of Spanish and German extraction, while she is Spanish and Irish decent," Bob said in an undertone to Al, as both men shook hands.

Al again met both Major Wood and Major Fox of the US Special Forces team. They both made some very guarded inquiries as to his health.

Al also reintroduced himself to Jaimie Perez, the Chief of Police in the Department of Cochabamba. He was a six foot blonde Prussian with a ramrod up his spine. Very trim and athletic in appearance, he had made a slight name change so that he would not be as easily recognized as a former German Army Colonel. The scuttlebutt that abounded about him was that he was strict but very fair in his dealings. They chatted for a few minutes and Al found him to be quite convivial. Jaime asked if he had been taking any more detours on the way to work lately. He was also happy to hear that Al had a permit for his pistol. There was not a word about the attempt on Al's life. It was obvious that Severeno had been reporting all the recent happenings to his chief.

Al looked over toward the corner table and there sat his recent acquaintances from the hotel bar, George Jordan and his wife Patricia. He had thought that they had left Cochabamba for Santa Cruz. Al walked over to their table.

"Good evening. I thought you were going to Santa Cruz. Must have been a fast trip. Did you fly?" Al queried.

"Why, ah, yes. We flew down there. It's a short flight," declared George.

Patricia smiled and said, "Our friends down there had left for Brazil, so we missed them."

George gave her a rather strained look.

Al noticed that the suit, although an expensive one had a bulge under the arm pit. He mused to himself: "I can only envision one thing that will make a bulge like that and it is not his wallet. I am beginning to suspect that he is either a cop or someone with something else on his mind."

They parted company with Al wondering, leaving him to questioning why they had changed their plans about driving to Santa Cruz and why she was obviously not being truthful.

What Al didn't know was that George and Patricia were from Buenas Aires, Argentina. In 1934, George and Giselle Jordan had left Argentina with their two children for their homeland in Canada. They were French Canadian citizens working in Argentina; therefore their children had dual citizenship. Both George Jr. and Patricia were raised speaking French, English and Spanish. Their parents died when the children were in their mid teens, leaving the twins to raise themselves.

They were not identical twins, but they were of one mind. They supported and protected each other's weaknesses and strengths. They both joined the Surete du Quebec. They had unblemished records. There was some conjecture that they may even have been lovers. Admittedly, they were a bit on the eccentric side. They traveled constantly from the time they were in their twenties. Their travels took them to all the major cities in Canada and the United States.

Some of the inspectors even harbored the thought that they worked together as a hit team, ridding the world of a number of unsavory characters. This, of course, was never proven, but remained in the minds of a number of law enforcement officials in Canada and the U. S.

Bob brushed his arm to introduce him to Mike Whiteman. Mike was a U. S. citizen living in Bolivia. His mother was North American while his father was English. Mike had a tin mine near Oruru in the Alta Plano He was six feet tall, with pale blond hair. He tipped the scales at 180 lbs. He was reputed to know every fishing hole in the Cordillera Oriental. His family owned a finca (ranch) about 20 miles from Cochabamba past Quillacollo. On top of all that, he was the primary hunting and fishing buddy of Bob's. Al and Mike immediately started swapping lies about fishing. It was so fraught with exaggerations that Mike and Bob finally laughingly invited Al on their next fishing expedition. They figured that anyone with fish stories as big as Al's had to be able to catch at least a minnow. Al left the time up to Bob.

The next person Al met was a six foot tall handsome Army Colonel. He was introduced to Colonel Ovando Tajada. They had already met at the alcalde's office. He smiled at Al and congratulated him on his staying alive. He was a graduate of the Bolivian Military Academy and carried himself like a true leader of armies. He was rumored to be an un-tiring womanizer; at least that was the rumor that followed him. Al watched him smile and embrace all the women with the brazo a brazo hug and kiss on each cheek until he was becoming reasonably sure that the rumors might have some substance. Al chatted with him for a few minutes until Al was accosted by Maggie Suarez.

"Al, I would like you to meet an old friend of mine," cooed Maggie. Al was prepared to meet yet another young woman, in a long line of single, and, some not so single, women that his various hostesses were always trying to pair him with. Any single male under fifty was fair game at these types of parties.

Maggie's voice had reached across the room to a small dark-haired woman, holding a glass of white wine. Her jet black hair cascaded down her back, almost to her waist. Al was prepared for a native Bolivian, but as she turned, with a friendly smile on her face, he saw her creamy complexion and dancing blue eyes.

Maggie continued with her introductions: "Carolina Longstreet, Al Provo. Al, this is Carrie. I'll leave you two to get acquainted." Maggie was already turning away, heading to another group by the bar.

"Hi, Maggie. How've you been? Haven't seen you in several weeks." Carrie smiled at Maggie, and flicked her eyes over to Al, as though she were about to give him a quick handshake, nod, and then move on to another group. But when she reached to touch him, she paused.

Al had also stopped, struck by her eyes, looking straight at him. He had a feeling that as soon as they touched, they would begin a long journey together. He wasn't sure he was ready for another woman in his life, actually _in_ his life.

They both reached toward each other at the same moment. Carrie spoke first.

"Al, is it? Is that short for Alfred, or Albert, or some exotic Bolivian name?"

"Not as exotic as Carolina. Is that North or South?" Al relaxed, as Maggie moved away from them, leaving Al and Carrie to parry with relaxing party talk.

"Actually, it's Albert. You were pretty close."

"And mine was from North Carolina, courtesy of a long ago ancestor who did the westward-ho thing."

Al realized he was still holding Carrie's hand, and she had made no move to break their contact. He lightly slid his hand up her arm, turning her toward the open patio door. She moved naturally with his touch, turning to speak softly to him.

"Will you be in Bolivia long?"

"Several months, helping Bob Adams on his project. How do you know the Adams?"

"Through their children, who attend The Institute Americano. I'm the principal." She smiled at Al, who did a fake grimace. "I'm especially fond of Agnes and their girls and boys. It's always great to have meals with such a lively family."

"I'd better behave, hadn't I?" he laughed. "But Maggie said you were from Cochabamba. You don't have an accent. So where are you really from?"

Carrie and Al had stepped through the patio door onto the paved outdoor area. Rhythmic music drifted across the lawn.

"My mother was Bolivian; my father was from Texas, where I was reared and schooled."

Al was ready to listen to her forever, but suddenly Maggie's voice cut through their conversation.

"Hey, you two. Come back inside. Carrie, the Colonel wants to talk with you – and Al, there seem to be a couple, the Barrets, who want to meet you."

Reluctantly, Al and Carrie moved back inside with Maggie. Just as Carrie walked away, she looked back at Al. "Another time?" He nodded.

CHAPTER 25

Al moved easily from group to group, fluently juggling both Spanish and the occasional Quechua phrase. He noticed Francois putting the make on a young housewife who was not at all interested. She let him know her disapproval of him, but he was hard to impress. He was being very difficult until the woman's husband (6'4", 240 pounds) rather belligerently told him to shove off. Francois ignored the husband until the husband grabbed him by the collar and the seat of his trousers and threw him headlong into the street. He did point out to Francois that the next time he laid a hand on his wife, he would go back to Canada in a body bag.

Al thought that was quite plain and to the point and decided that he didn't want any piece of that action.

Most of the husbands in the place decided that the irate husband deserved a drink, and congratulated him on ridding the place of the trouble maker.

It was interesting that neither Pierre Lamont nor Ian MacDonald stepped into the breach to save their fellow Canadian from bodily harm. They must be as fed up with him as was everyone else.

Will Barret and his wife Arlene were charming company and did their best to make Al feel like one of the group. They told him about their daughter Gail and the fact that she attended school at The Institute Americano and they could not say enough good things about Carrie.

Will, the Project Engineer from Georgia, was 6'3" tall. He stood out in this area where the average height is about 5'5". His brown hair was thinning prematurely to a bald pate. He looked like a line backer for the Falcons. He had worked on several tunnels in the Atlanta area, namely the Atlanta Sewage tunnel, driven with a TBM. Fortunately, Will had a very calm and controlled demeanor, never seeming to get irritated or upset.

Maggie and Juan caught up with Al and told him that they would like very much for him to attend their party next Saturday evening at their home. They said there would be about ten couples there and if Al wanted to bring someone they would enjoy the company.

Before he could say that he had no one to bring, Maggie the match maker suggested that Al might ask Carrie. Maggie thought that Carrie would be happy to attend with him.

That sounded good to him, but now Al had to corner her again to ask her. Unfortunately she had already left the party and returned to her home.

"Now what do I do?" Al wondered.

Father Tim was still standing so Al cornered him for some conversation.

He told Al of a story that he had heard on the grape vine about the illustrious Colonel. The Colonel had left with a willing damsel on his arm about an hour ago, so it was safe to talk about him.

"Not too long ago, the Colonel was met at his house by his usual contingent of body guards and vehicles for a ride to his office. It was about 8:00 AM when the retinue drove up to his house. The Colonel was late, as usual, and walked hurriedly to the lead car. Just as he was about to get into the car, he recalled that he had left his brief case and all his important notes in his bedroom. He dashed back into the house just in time to hear the car that he was to ride in blow up. That is the way I heard it," said Father Tim. "That guy has more lives than a cat."

The party wound down about one in the morning, so everyone left for home.

Al stopped by the Adams' residence for a cup of coffee after the party.

"Agnes, if I were to ask Carrie to go to the Suarez party next Saturday, do you think she would accept, and how do I find her to ask?" Al asked.

"I doubt that you would have any trouble, as I think she is interested in you. Let me tell you a little about her," Agnes continued.

"Carrie Longstreet is the daughter of land rich hacendados, or land owners as you would call them, on her mother's side. Her father, Mica Longstreet, a U.S. citizen, was working in Bolivia developing the tin mines in the Altiplano near Oruru. He made numerous trips to Cochabamba to purchase materials and to get some rest from the higher altitude of Oruru. He met Carolina's mother, Alicia Zavalla y Peron, at an afternoon tea during one of his visits to Cochabamba and became enamored by her smile.

Alicia in turn found that she was deeply attached to this swashbuckling Gringo, and decided that he was to be her husband, no matter what. She managed to ditch her Duena, her chaperone, long enough to get Mica to propose. They were married against the better judgment of her family. They were worried that Mica was trying to work his way into the Peron fortune. They obviously had not done their homework, as Mica's family had the same opinion of Alicia's being a gold digger.

The Longstreet family stretched back to North Carolina during the Revolution. They had moved west after the Civil War and had made their fortune in cattle, land and, lately, in oil. Actually, this was the combining of two rather large fortunes. After their marriage, the Longstreets lived in Bolivia for another year while Mica completed his work on the tin mine. They then moved to Texas where Carrie was born on a ranch owned by the Longstreets."

"Carolina was schooled in private schools in the United States, and for her university studies, she attended undergraduate and graduate schools at Tulane, receiving her PhD in education from the University of Georgia. She married a university classmate, and decided not to have a family until they were better entrenched in their chosen professions. Her husband died in an automobile accident a year later."

"After the deaths of her husband and her father she decided to return to Bolivia to be near her mother. She re-took her family name of Longstreet after the death of her husband as is the general custom among Spanish women. She returned to Bolivia to find that a goodly portion of the Zavalla family fortune had been eroded by the Agrarian Revolution in 1952.

There was still a substantial nest egg, but nothing like what she was raised to expect. This was of little importance to her as she had inherited a very large fortune from her parents in land and oil properties. She soon became bored sitting around and attending teas with her mother's friends. The Institute Americano board of directors called on her to apply as Principal for the twelve year school. This was a Methodist school that had been in existence for some 100 years, and was very prestigious in Bolivia. Carolina took the position and found it to be very rewarding. She is one of my best friends here in Bolivia. There are no men in her life."

After this biography Agnes stopped for a short breath.

She then said, "I'll arrange a dinner party Wednesday evening so that you two can get to know each other a little better."

That seemed to be more than a little about Carrie, but it made Carrie that much more interesting.

Bob and Agnes dropped Al off at the hotel after inviting him to dinner on Sunday afternoon about six.

Agnes asked Bob, "I have a feeling that you haven't told me everything about Al. He seems to be a lot more than what he admits to."

Bob replied, "I don't know any more than you do except that he and Severeno were attacked on the road to the job and Al's fast reflexes enabled him to shoot back killing one and wounding the other. They then went after the gang and their leader. It seems, according to the story by Severeno, the bad guys all ended up dead. It's a little improbable that it was just luck as he is trying to tell me; I think he has had a lot more training than he lets on about. Serious training I mean. Al is also becoming a bit paranoid after the punctured brake line."

CHAPTER 26

Al hired a taxi after breakfast on Sunday and had him drive up the mountain to the new Lago Bolivar. It was a beautiful lake surrounded by high peaks all around and a major series of falls just below the dam for a total of almost 900 feet. The lake was very serene and calm. The driver told him that they could catch trout as long as 36 inches. They drove past an old Catholic church and a small village that was located at the upper end of the lake. Then they started back up the long grade with four hairpin curves that led to the top of the mountain pass at 12.000 feet. This ride had been awe inspiring, scenic and surprisingly educational. Terraces for potatoes and corn climbed up and down the sides of the mountain. Al laughingly suggested that the reason for planting on the sides of the mountain was so that the potatoes could be rolled down hill to market.

The taxi driver told him that a number of years ago the U.S. AID people had sent a number of corn planters to Cochabamba to provide a more modern method of corn planting. The joke, though, was two pronged. One was that the corn planters needed tractors to pull them. No tractors. The second was that the corn planting machines were intended for use on reasonably flat terrain. All the corn is planted on very steep side hills.

The corn planters were rapidly stock piled along side the road. No one borrowed any parts from them as they were too complicated for use any place else. To top this act of brilliance, some one in the US State department felt it would be of great help to the indigenous population if road signs and village signs were installed throughout the area. This was very promptly accomplished. All the signs were in phonetic Quechua. The literacy rate was something like 25% among the cholos. So! Who was to read them?

The taxi arrived at the Adams's door at six, just in time for dinner. Al knocked on the door and found that Agnes had blindsided him. He was greeted by no other than Carrie. She wasn't supposed to be there until Wednesday evening dinner. It was a very pleasant surprise, seeing her smiling face. Al was a little embarrassed when she greeted him with a brazo a brazo (a hug with pat on each other's back, sometimes a friendly kiss on each cheek) just like he was an old friend or family member. He did not realize that she had already decided that he was to be the man in her life.

They had a most enjoyable dinner with a lot of conversation and good after dinner drinks.

Carrie did allow Al time to ask her to go to the Suarez party next Saturday evening as his date. She was most agreeable. Agnes informed him that they would pick him up at the hotel, and then pick up Carrie at her home.

Al's intuition told him that somehow the whole arrangement of meeting and dating Carrie was conceived and orchestrated by Agnes and her friends.

"Beware matchmaking women," Al mused.

In spite of his premonition that he had been outflanked, he enjoyed the company and the light hearted banter from Carrie. All things must come to an end, thus the dinner had to finish, and they all had to call it a night. Al arranged to pick Carrie up at her house late Monday afternoon to take an excursion of the area and a late dinner at a local restaurant. He found a taxi and escorted Carrie to her home. She gave him a hug and disappeared into the house before either of them could screw up the moment.

Al rested rather fitfully through the night thinking about that wonderful smile. He realized he was hooked, but what the hell, he only had one life.

CHAPTER 27

Monday morning arrived and with it his usual aches and pains getting upright for the day. He showered and shaved, dressed and made ready for the day. Al braced himself for the ride up the mountain with Severeno, hoping that things would go right today. He knew that he would feel better about the day as soon as he had his morning cup of coffee and some breakfast at the mess hall.

His proclivity toward paranoia kept him wondering about all the stories he had been hearing about the Colonel and his ability to survive numerous attacks, and the odds on LaBatt creating more trouble among the miners and what the result of his actions would be. He also was worried about the potential of finding good rock once they had advanced ahead of the TBM.

He was also beginning to question the advisability of getting to know Carrie any better. He seemed to have a major crush on her. What if she decided to become involved with him? They were from different ends of the universe, Al a confirmed bachelor always on the move with a questionable life behind him and she a confirmed educator in a foreign country. The big question was: where would this all end?

This inner conflict faded as soon as he arrived on the tunnel site. He looked up Bob in the mess hall and asked," How is everything going this morning - no catastrophes, no earth quakes or revolutions yet today?"

Bob said, "The Saturday advance in the tunnel was twelve feet, adding up to 100 feet, or half way to the goal of head of the TBM. We seem to be getting out of the woods on this problem."

Al nodded his head and took some messages from Bob from the States. They stated that the temporary Master Mechanic, Ozzie Chippendale, would arrive on site the end of the month. The temporary Tunnel Superintendent, Toni Parsonopolis, and an expert TBM driver named Hans Gerber would both be on site inside of two weeks.

"This a good start for the day. It looks like things will work out if we can get the TBM unstuck," Bob smiled. "Do you want to go to the tunnel to see how they are doing this morning?"

"That sounds like a great idea to me," Al replied.

They went into the tunnel with George Padilla and Envero Aguilar where they explained that the crew had just finished drilling out the face and were starting to load dynamite in the heading. They watched the loading process and left the tunnel.

"Fire in the hole," shouted Envero, when the tunnel face was loaded and ready for blasting.

They counted the delays as they went off and the explosion created a large WHOOMPH. They then waited for about twenty minutes for the tunnel to air out before going back in. The tunnel had cut clean with minimal bootleg (unbroken rock along the ribs). They had pulled a four foot round.

"Good going," Al told Envero.

It was now about noon, so Bob and Al went to the mess hall for lunch. Both Bob and Al decided that this afternoon would be as good a time as any to drive over to the North portal to see what need be done for access.

This trip was much easier to talk about than it was to do. To get to the North portal 20,000 feet away through the tunnel required that they travel about 15 miles around the mountain. Before future access with equipment, they would have to construct an access road. That did not seem like much on paper; however the route would traverse very steep slopes and make innumerable hairpin turns. The hairpins would have to be large enough to allow the passage of heavily loaded trucks.

They left with Jesus so that Bob and Al would be able to give their thoughts as to how they would be able to pioneer the haul road to the North Portal when the time came. The road they had to travel was actually a llama track that led through canyons, along streams and steep mountain sides.

Al suggested, "This is a refresher course in map reading and navigating in rough terrain."

Al said, "Happily we will not be bothered by trees as we were above the tree line. Some poor SOB had worked his butt off staking out an alignment. I'll bet you that the survey was done with a hand level and a Brunton compass."

Fortunately they did have the survey stakes to follow. Some were well below and others were well above the precipitous route they were traversing. Some of this route extended to over 15,000 foot elevation.

They drove the Jeep part of the way over an old Inca cobblestone road that was so steep that the only way to stay on the eight foot wide road and to make the switch backs was to alternately drive forward with the jeep then back the jeep down the next section of road. This was a spine jarring ride as the Incas did not have the wheel, so did not need a smooth road. They needed stair steps so their runners could travel up and down the mountains. This particular road ran from the Altiplano to the Beni near Santa Cruz. By the time they arrived at the North Portal, Al was convinced that he would rather walk back. The trip of 15 miles had required four tortuous hours. Based on their travel in, they might be able to get back to the office by 8:30 that night.

Building the access road was going to be a real challenge, not only to build it, but just to stay on the side of the mountain. There were places where vertical rock cliffs projected out over the proposed road alignment.

Al pointed out, "Those areas will have to be drilled and shot to form half an arch with a roadway on the bench. Other areas will require very high retaining walls or retained earth systems to allow the construction of a road bed. All of this is very time consuming and expensive."

They thought that they had better take a good look tomorrow at the estimate for this piece of work. There must be an easier way to get there.

They returned to the South Portal by back tracking the way they had come. Fortunately they did not have to explore questionable routes this time; they just followed the proven way. The return travel took just under three hours.

They were glad to get back to a decent road and head back to Cochabamba.

They were both tired after that ride so they repaired to their respective living quarters.

Al called Carrie, "I am running late, but I'll be by your place in about thirty minutes."

Al took a taxi and was met at the door by Carrie. She took one look at him and thought: "He looks completely out of it - maybe we should just take it easy this evening, let him rest a little."

"Al, you look like you had a very bad day, what happened?" asked Carrie.

"We decided that things were going too easily, so Bob and I drove the access road alignment. We ended riding or I should say bouncing around in that Land Cruiser for about seven hours, I am not sure but I may have a number of fractured vertebrae as well as cracked ribs. Do you mind if we eat out and make it a reasonably early evening so I can recuperate?"

They decided that a quiet dinner at a local Italian restaurant would be fine as they both had to work the next day.

CHAPTER 28

Morning found him well rested and ready to take on the world. He met Severeno at the curb outside the hotel and they headed for the job.

About the only exciting things along the road were a few conejos (rabbits) that looked more like hamsters. They had short ears, but Severeno claimed that they were rabbits. At least he thought they were good to eat. Al could see no redeeming value to the short fat rodents.

They had just made the cumbre when they met a herd of alpacas crossing the road in front of them. There were ten or more of them. The only difference between them and the llama was that the llama was larger, and it appeared to Al that the alpaca have longer wool. Other than that small difference they acted the same to the herders' hoots and whistles. The llamas were bred as beasts of burden. They were both very aloof animals, distant relatives of the camel.

Just beyond the next switchback past the alpaca crossing they had a flat tire. Severeno climbed out of the Jeep and as he did they heard a vehicle leave the next switchback at high speed.

"That is strange. Why would anyone be up around the next corner?" thought Al.

Severeno had finished replacing the tire with the spare and bent to examine the damage. He straightened up with a worried look on his face.

"Senor Provo, the tire was hit by a bullet. Someone was shooting at us but missed and hit the tire. Let's take a look up around the corner, see what we can find."

They drove to the next switchback, about 200 yards and found a large boulder on the side of the road.

"Look Senor Provo, there are some boot tracks and an empty cartridge case on the ground. Those boot tracks weren't made by a campesino because they don't have boots. It must have been a Gringo," said Severeno.

The cartridge case was .22 caliber, an easily obtained caliber at any store in Bolivia.

"Well not much we can do here, so let's go on to the job, We had better think about who that was that tried to ambush us." said Al.

After all that excitement, they drove on to the office and Al immediately headed to the mess hall to relate the happenings to Bob.

Domingo told him as they were eating, "We now have a total of ninety feet of drift excavated. That leaves us with a total of eighty-eight feet to go."

Bob suggested, "If the rock will stay put and not cave in, we should start trying to pull three six foot rounds per day for eighteen feet per day. We should be able to handle that. That means working out in front of the ribs about six feet. Just have the crew be very careful."

Bob looked thoughtful as he finished his coffee.

"How are we doing uncovering the trailing floor of the TBM? Can we start repairs next week?" Bob asked.

Domingo replied, "Why don't we go to the tunnel and see just how far they are on the recovery?"

They all paraded to the tunnel portal and went in to the trailing floor. About one hundred feet of the three hundred foot long structure was uncovered. The demolished tunnel support ribs had been removed for scrap and new ribs had been re-installed. The structural components appeared to be over designed and fortunately were reasonably intact. The structure would need only minimal repairs for the structural components. It appeared that the re-mining around the trailing floor and the TBM would advance rapidly enough so that part of the work would not slow down re-starting the main tunnel advance.

"Why don't we go back to the office and work on our access road problem?" Al then asked.

The project copy of the bid estimate that the company had made was pulled out of the job files. It looked like the estimating group had done their homework. The estimate had allowed sufficient time and money to build the road. The schedule, though, did indicate that the work would have to start within the next two months to provide the road when needed. Al knew that the road building equipment was on its way from the States and should arrive within the month.

"Looks like Domingo will have his hands full just getting that road through. It may be fortunate that we have a temporary tunnel superintendent on the way here. I'm not convinced that he will be temporary, maybe for one year at least," Al told Bob.

"It's beginning to look like you're right," Bob said. "I hope he doesn't have any plans for a year or so."

They finished out the afternoon and headed down the mountain to Cochabamba.

CHAPTER 29

Al had dressed and headed to the Adams' house for another great home cooked meal. He stopped on the way and bought a couple of bottles of wine and a bottle of Scotch. These purchases could not repay their hospitality, but it would show that his heart was in the right place.

He was again greeted by four charming ladies at the Adams' door. First there was Carrie, then Agnes, with Rita and Sarah working their way into the greeting by poking around both Carrie and Agnes. It seemed that just because he had become friendly with Carrie, the two girls decided that he was suddenly a VIP. The two boys sort of yawned and then ignored him, as he was cutting into their time with Carrie. "Too bad guys - go find someone your own age," he thought to himself.

They had a very nice civilized family dinner. After dinner the younger set wanted to play board games. After much pleading by Rita and Sarah, Agnes gave in and enlisted all of them to play. She did limit playing Monopoly to one hour so that the old folks could relax for a while.

After the games Al had an opportunity to talk with Carrie a bit. He continued to find her a very good conversationalist as well as very charming. He was growing to enjoy her company more as time went by.

Al asked, "Would you care take in a movie Friday evening and then out to dinner on Saturday evening? We could escape this bunch and might even be able to hold hands without one of them peeking around the door."

Carrie said," I would love to go to a movie with you next Friday evening and out for a fancy dinner on Saturday evening. I agree that a little privacy would be in order. I most certainly would like some quiet time alone with you."

The get-together started to fade as tired people started to make excuses about having to go to work in the morning. Al offered to take Carrie back to her house, and was rewarded by a big smile from Carrie.

They took a taxi and upon arriving at her house Carrie asked, "Would you like to come in for a nightcap before going back to your hotel?"

"Yes, I would enjoy that," Al almost blurted out. Hee had been hoping she would ask.

Her house was a turn of the century structure that had been her mother's before she died. Carrie had inherited it as well as the house full of antique furniture. The house had a large foyer, a living room and a dinning room with the kitchen opening off of it. The second story had five bedrooms and two bath rooms. The building was of brick with white painted stucco. The interior finish was in very ornately carved walnut along the walls as well as the stairs to the second floor. It was a very comfortable home.

Carrie served Scotch on the rocks and a variety of snacks. Carrie was still very curious about Al's background, so after a plate of snacks and several glasses of Scotch on the rocks , she decided to ask a lot more questions than she had before.

"Al, I think you know most of my history, what about you?" Carrie asked. "Are you married, or do you have someone in San Francisco? Where were you raised and how did you get into the construction business? Where did you go to school, and tell me something about your parents and your brothers and sisters."

"Whoa! Slow down, I can't answer everything at one time, but I was raised in Northern Vermont, I have no siblings and my parents have both passed on. I drifted around after the University of Vermont and joined the Army during the Korean Peace Action I went to OCS and was commissioned a 2nd Lt. After I was discharged, I went to work for a contractor. No, I am not married and no, I do not have someone in San Francisco."

Carrie decided to let the inquiry drop - for the time being. She thought a minute, then moved on to an entirely different subject.

"Has anyone told you how Agnes first met the American women here in Cochabamba?, Well several of the women dropped by after she had moved in to their house and introduced themselves and informed her of the importance of their husbands in the general scheme of things. Their importance did not interest Agnes. Agnes was then asked if she played bridge and was flat out told that it was the major thing in Cochabamba's social life and that if one did not play, then they were not in with the social set. Agnes politely informed them that, no, she did not play bridge and that she came to Bolivia to meet Bolivians and not to sit around a card table. This did not go over too well, but that did not bother Agnes."

"She shortly thereafter organized a group of the women to cook food weekly to be taken to the local orphanage. They cooked up about ten gallons of spaghetti with meat sauce and took it to the children. The orphans ranged from one year to about ten years of age. Children older than that would be taken by their family out of the orphanage to help in the fields. There were about one-hundred children being fed on about $1.00 per month per child. Some of the children had been born while their mothers were working in the corn fields or potato patches. These children belonged in the new Patino Orphanage. They were not there because the orphanage had been built, furnished and then due to political differences had been locked up, unused. That is a whole other story."

They talked way beyond a reasonable hour until she called Al a taxi so he could go back to the hotel.

Carrie asked, "Would you like to drive up to the lake Saturday afternoon and have a picnic?"

Al replied, "Yes, I think that would be very nice. What time?"

"How about around 1:30?"

She kissed him good night and this time it was nothing like a sisterly kiss. He left in the taxi feeling ten feet tall.

CHAPTER 30

Wednesday morning was the same as all the others. It was beginning to be a challenge for Al to roll out of bed at an early hour to ride to the job with Severeno.

"I have noticed a lot of cactus plants along the road with big flowers and what looks like fruit. What are they?" Al asked Severeno.

"Ah, yes, those are Toombas or flowers of the cactus plant. We cut the spines off of the fruit and cook it or eat it raw. It is very good."

"Severeno, I have seen potatoes in the fields with white, yellow, red and blue flowers. Are they all different kinds of potatoes?" Al asked.

"The potatoes are of many different kinds and sizes. Some are only a few inches in diameter and they vary up to eight or ten inches in diameter. We have sweet potatoes as well. All potatoes originated in South America. The cholos have been raising potatoes for over three thousand years. In fact chunu has been found in three thousand year old ruins. Chunu is a dehydrated potato that is made by leaving the potatoes out in the open at night to freeze then pulverizing them with bare feet and then re-freezing at night until all the moisture has been dried out of them. When you want to eat them, all you have to do is add some water and heat them. Of course by this time the potatoes are black and not very appetizing to look at, but you get used to them."

All this education during a forty minute ride was a bit staggering.

They met a stake bed truck about half way up the mountain, just past the third switchback. The driver's side of the truck was head first into the side of the mountain with the front end badly smashed in. The rear of the truck was at an angle across the road, completely blocking access. A half dozen cholas were congregating around the front of the truck, all very excited.

Al and Severeno stopped the jeep and walked over to find out what was going on. The truck had lost its brakes and had been driven along the side wall of the road in a futile attempt to stop from going over the mountain into the canyon. Unfortunately, one of the cholos had been riding on the front fender of the truck on the driver's side. He had been wedged between the truck fender and the side wall for the last several hundred feet and was horribly crushed and torn up. The cholos covered him with an old burlap potato sack, and then proceeded to move the truck away from the bank so that Al and Severeno could drive on by.

They had met a number of other stake bed trucks full of campesinos with the goods that they hoped to trade or sell at the market today and tomorrow. These goods included but were not limited to potatoes, maize, squash, chicha, and hand crafted items such as ponchos, sweaters and shirts.

When they arrived at the camp, Al went directly to the mess hall where he told the group about the truck accident.

"It's never easy to be confronted with death. Human life here in the Andes seems to be fragile, somehow."

There was a murmuring of agreement around the tables, and then everyone was quiet for a few minutes, drinking coffee.

Al continued his breakfast in the mess hall with Bob and the rest of the crew. A large cup of Bolivian coffee was just what he needed as he went over the previous day's work with Bob, Jesus, and all the engineering staff, as well as the inspectors. This day, which had otherwise started as a nice sunlit morning, had ended with a soul chilling ride up the mountain.

"How did the crew do yesterday, Jesus?" Al asked.

"They made twelve feet advance in the tunnel. That leaves us with seventy-six feet to go. The rock is still too badly fractured in the crown to allow us to go to 6'-0" rounds. We will have to play it by ear."

"Just work with the rock, but don't over extend our capabilities to the point of being dangerous." Bob said. "How are we doing on clearing the TBM trailing floor?"

"We cleared another 30 feet. The structure is not damaged, but we will have to replace some of the air and water lines. I don't think that the power supply lines have been damaged," replied Jesus.

"We should be getting in the road building equipment in about a week. Have you lined up your crews so we will be ready to go? That job will be a real challenge for you and the crews. We will have to work 12 hour shifts six days a week to get it finished on schedule," Bob told Jesus.

The day was spent planning their work and the needs for both the tunnel and the access road.

They worked on equipment needs as well as supplies and the logistics of having everything on site when needed.

Al rode back down the mountain with Severeno driving. They had no misadventures on this trip, however did see a number of campesinos walking, or possibly staggering, along the road. They must have been partying most of the day as they were glassy eyed. Al and Severeno did see one campesino being beat on by a rather large campesina. Severeno thought that the husband must have been out with some younger woman. They just could not tolerate any quantity of chicha. One or two glasses and they were gone for the day.

Al arrived at the hotel with only one thing in mind. A hot shower and a change of clothes so he would look reasonably kept up when he hit the bar for a before dinner drink.

The first people that he saw were George and Patricia Jordan. They invited him over to their table for a drink.

"How are you doing today? We didn't have much of a chance to talk at the cocktail party the other night," George offered, "What are you doing here in Cochabamba? Rumors suggest that you may be connected with the tunnel project. Is that right?"

Al answered, "I'm just a visiting fireman working with Bob Adams, on some details on the Tunnel Boring Machine. You seem to be very busy tourists. Are you from Montreal by any chance? You have that twang in your speech."

"No, no, we're from Buenas Aires," George answered very emphatically. "We're just on a short vacation. We visit each part of South America for several weeks each year. We had a Canadian teacher who taught us English. That's where our accents come from."

The three of them lied to each other a while longer until Al begged off, with the story that he had an appointment to meet someone.

It seems strange to Al, who thought to himself: "I still seemed to detect a French accent rather than a Castilian inflection that would be typical of an Argentine. I think they might be Argentine, but I would bet the farm that they were raised in Quebec province with Canadian French being their family language. They'd have picked up English and Castilian as added languages. Oh! It is none of my business so I will let it drop."

Al stopped at the front desk to see if he had any messages. Carrie had left a message saying that she had a wonderful time last evening and was looking forward to the movie on Friday evening.

"Looks like my good looks and charm could well get me into trouble, but such nice trouble," thought Al.

He went to the dining room and noted that the Jordans had left. He was about to sit down when he heard a familiar voice calling to him. It was Maggie, sitting by herself. She motioned for Al to approach her table and said that she needed company.

"Where's Juan? I am surprised that he would let you out of his sight. Sitting here alone you will have every unattached male in Cochabamba trying to hit on you," Al said jokingly.

"That is why I asked you to sit with me. All the guys will think that I have a protector," she laughed. "So how's it going with Carrie? I think she has a crush on you. Saw her this morning and all she could talk about was Al this and Al that. You have sure made a hit with her."

"I think that she could well become something quite special to me."

"You do know that she hasn't had a date since her husband died almost thirteen years ago. She came down here right after he died to be with her mother. Her mother died three years ago and she's been alone since then. Most of the single and not so single guys in town have been hitting on her, even my husband, but none of them even got to kiss her on the door step. So! Here comes the Gringo Engineer friend of the Adams, and voila, she starts to have wild thoughts, like a man in her life. She's not the only female around here to have wild thoughts about you," Maggie smirked.

"If what you say is true then I guess I had better stay up on the mountain and keep track of the TBM. There really isn't much more to my life than work and a few drinks of Scotch. I travel and move around too much for any woman to become attached to me."

"Al, don't kid yourself; while the cat is away, the mice will play. Let's finish our dinner and the wine and I'll prove to you that this mouse is ready and willing to play," Maggie said very seriously. "I've been interested since we first met on the Prado.

Al pushed his drink around the table, all the while thinking to himself: "God, what a night. I think I'd better keep away from Maggie. Juan might not be very understanding."

CHAPTER 31

Severeno was, as usual, waiting for Al at the curb in front of the hotel. He drove another calm ride to the job site.

Both Bob and Jesus were at the breakfast table sipping on their first cup of coffee for the morning. They always drank a small demitasse of coffee. Al accused them of being weak, couldn't stand good coffee.

Jesus said, "The tunnel crews had advanced twenty-four feet yesterday for a total of 172 feet, leaving another twenty-eight feet to go to until they are back on the tunnel alignment." Clearing of the trailing floor was nearly complete. Another quarter mile of road work had been pioneered and ready for rough grading.

Al was sitting with Bob in the mess hall for lunch when he asked Bob about Patino.

"Last evening Carrie told me about the meals that Agnes organized for the orphans. She told me that there is a new children's hospital and orphanage here in Cochabamba funded by Patino but never opened. She said there was a political problem. Can you enlighten me?"

Bob said, "The story around here is that Simon Patino is claimed to be a cholo but his family claims that he was descended from Europeans. Legend has it that he was a shop keeper in the Altiplano and grub-staked some of the miners. He was fired from his job for being so generous. One of the miners that he loaned food and money to did not pay up, so Patino took over the mine claim. This just happened to be the richest vein of tin ever found in Bolivia. Patino ended up owning most of the tin mines in the country and it has been claimed that at the outset of World War II, he was one of the richest men in the world.

"He had smelters in France and in Germany. He apparently became very political and after the revolution in 1952 his mines were nationalized. He was at odds with the Bolivian government before 1952 before they nationalized his mines. His son became politically active after his father died in Buenas Aires, Argentina in 1947. His son apparently built the orphanage but had not come to terms with the government."

"Patino was a native of Cochabamba and had built a mansion in the center of the city. In 1964 Charles de Gaulle visited Bolivia. He was an old friend of the Patinos. He stayed in the Patino mansion. The altitude of LaPaz was considered to be detrimental to his health so he landed in

Cochabamba. The street leading to the fenced Patino mansion was of graded gravel. This of course would not do, so another street paved with asphalt was torn up and re-laid on the street to the Patino mansion."

Bob was chuckling as he told Al of this last bit of trivia.

Saturday morning Al, with his usual bacon and fried eggs at the camp mess hall, listened to Bob and Jesus, as they reported that the final four feet of access tunnel had been driven.

Bob said, "Now we can start a short section of the main tunnel to restart the TBM. We can also start drilling ahead to cut-off grout the water. The rock looks better and needs less support. Not only that, but the miners are getting a rhythm now and are better able to drill and set ribs in a reasonable time. The rescue of the trailing floor should be completed the first of the week."

"How is the access road pioneering doing?"

Jesus informed them that it had advanced about a mile, so that when the heavy highway equipment arrives they will have plenty of room to work in.

Bob and Al both went into the tunnel on a quick inspection trip and then walked out on the pioneer road to see how that looked.

They both made a few observations to Jesus that might make his tasks a bit easier.

CHAPTER 32

Al changed into khakis and hiking boots, then took a taxi to Carrie's house. Carrie greeted Al at the door with a very warm kiss and hug, as though he had been gone for weeks.

She had a picnic lunch packed in a big picnic hamper.

"Here, put this in the back of my car and we will go up to the lake to do a little hiking, have a picnic and just enjoy the day," Carrie said.

Al put the picnic hamper into the back of a red 1962 Toyota Land Cruiser. This little four wheel drive could deliver them any place they wanted to go.

Carrie came out of the house dressed in khaki trousers and shirt as well as leather field boots. Al could not help but notice as she slid a Colt .45 auto under her seat. She informed him that all well dressed women packed a .45 when they went out in the country.

The new road to Santa Cruz was still under construction and had not yet been paved. They drove past the military post on the outskirts of Cochabamba, past Sacaba, and through several other villages with all their adobe block casas. There was always a church in the middle of these villages. All of the casas had adobe walls around them for the pigs and sheep. Al and Carrie could see the drying strips of charke (Quechua for dried meat). This was originally llama meat, and it was believed that it was where they get the word jerky for dried meat in North America.

They worked their way up the tortuous mountain road to the pass.

Carrie said, "In the winter mornings there will be granular snow on the ground, but it will be gone by noon as soon as the sun comes up."

The pass was at an elevation of 12,000 feet. The mountain reared up over them to 14,000 feet and the canyons below them drop precipitously to 10,000 feet. The road was of loose gravel 14 to 20 feet wide and had no guard rails. It was obviously a road that required the drivers' attention.

There was not much in the way of scenery at the pass as there were abrupt mountains both behind them and ahead of them. The mountainside was desolate of vegetation, nothing but dried grass.

"As soon as we pass through to the other side we will begin to see an opening in the mountains to the North," Carrie said.

A long switchback came into view stretching down the mountain to an elevation of 10,000 feet. The road veered off to the left into a broad flat valley. The first thing they saw was the village of Colomi, just upstream of the lake. The village had two dozen casas and a single Catholic church beside the road. The stream flowed alongside the road until it emptied into the lake. They drove on along the lake on the new road to a lookout over the series of falls dropping about 900 feet. The mountain jungle started just below the crest of the falls. Al had been to this point a week ago in a rented taxi.

Carrie said, "This is where we get out and hike up over the mountain to the East of the dam and road. The top of our climb is at 12,000 feet. The view from here is spectacular. You can see the cloud banks from the Amazon backing up to the mountain range at about 10,000 feet." They could almost reach out and touch them. Mountain peaks rose sharply up like giant fingers pointing to heaven. The green mountain jungle spread out like a giant carpet. The mahogany trees crowned out over the lower growths, hiding them from the sun.

"Carrie, this is the most beautiful spot I have seen for many years. I'm really enjoying the scenery and the wonderful company. Thank you very much," said Al. "I hope we can do this again."

Al engulfed her shoulders with his arm, pulling her to him. He felt her body shudder as he kissed her passionately. They decided that they had better get back down the hill before they got into more trouble than they were ready for at this time.

They hiked back down the hill to the waiting Land Cruiser and their picnic lunch. They retrieved their lunch and went to the side of the lake where they sat down to eat. They could see fishermen out on the lake casting for the trout that are reputed to be in these waters. Occasionally, one of the fishermen would pull in a large trout, and then continue to cast once more. Carrie and Al were like two giddy kids setting there on the lake side, enjoying the quiet and the fantastic setting of this area.

Al could not resist the temptation of putting his arm around Carrie's shoulders and drawing her near to him. "I could get used to this; it's very nice holding you in my arms and dreaming of a long wonderful future for the two of us. I'm afraid I'm falling for you."

"I'd like that very much," murmured Carrie as she snuggled up to him to feel the warmth of his body through his shirt.

They eventually packed up their picnic hamper and headed back to Cochabamba. They were both very contented after this idealistic afternoon.

Carrie's family had owned the ranch at the head of the new lake. They'd lost that during the 1952 change of government. The vacant buildings still stood in solitude.

They stopped at the small Catholic church in Colomi where an old friend of Carrie's was pastor. Al was introduced to Father Guido Bertonelli, formerly of Padua, Italy. They talked for some time and the question of how long the good father had been in Colomi came up.

"I have been here for thirty years trying to convert these people to be good Catholics. I feel that I have failed my mission and am to retire and return to Italy next month," Father Guido stated.

"What makes you think you've failed?" Al asked.

"In thirty years of working with them and preaching the gospel, I know that they sit in church and worship God, but as soon as they get back to their casas they go inside and on one wall is the figure of Christ and on the other wall is the figure of Inti (the Inca sun god). They direct their prayers to Inti. These people just don't trust our blue eyed savior. I am tired and know that I should leave them to a younger priest, so I am going home," said Father Guido.

They decided on the return to town to go out to the Chinese restaurant for an evening meal. It was Al's observation that no matter where one travels in this world, or how remote the village is, one will always find a Chinese and or an Italian restaurant. They ordered hot and sour soup, fried won ton, pork fried rice, deep fried pork, pot stickers and Peking duck. They were both adept with chop sticks.

After dinner they returned to Carrie's house for a night cap, and to make plans for Sunday, when they recalled that they had been invited to the Adams' for a dinner party. They were to show up there at two. That more or less settled the problem of Sunday.

"I will be by about one so that we can go from here," Al said.

Al finally dragged himself away sometime late in the evening, regretting the fact that he had to leave someone with whom he had so much in common and who was rapidly coming to mean so much to him.

CHAPTER 34

Sunday morning found him sleeping late. He went to the dining room for a late breakfast, and then about one he caught a taxi for Carrie's house. They went to the Adams', and found themselves a bit early by Bolivian standards.

To their surprise they found that this was to be a rather large buffet type meal with everyone spreading out around the house.

They bumped into Mike Whiteman, a neighbor of the Adams. He and Bob were plotting a fishing trip to Jatun Rumi (Quechua for large rock) about forty miles up and over Mt Tunari. This trip would take about four hours if everything went right. This was to be their third attempt at fishing in the stream there. The last time Mike, Bob and Lucio Esparenza had started on this expedition was about four months ago. They had gotten to the pass at 15,000 feet at six in the evening, when the alternator on the Jeep gave out. Being stubborn they decided to keep going, at times without head lights, driving by moon light.

The temperature dropped to about 20 degrees Fahrenheit so that all water was solid ice. They had to sleep curled up in the Jeep, shivering until morning. The road was an old Inca cobble stone construction that was designed and constructed for runners and not for wheels. There were an unbelievable number of switch backs that required that they drive up to the turn then back the Jeep to the next turn.

They finally arrived at their favorite fishing stream only to find that the locals had been fishing with dynamite and had temporarily cleaned out all the fish. To top it off, Bob dropped through the deep grass beside the stream into a hole about four feet deep. During the fall he hit his ribs against the dirt on the side of the hole and fractured several ribs. A large bottle of brandy saved the day. Several hours later some fishermen drove by in a Jeep and after much negotiation Mike talked them into alternately switching batteries, charging Bob's and allowing everyone to get back to civilization, without fish.

Agnes sort of embarrassed them about that trip so Mike came up with another scheme. This scheme has to be the wildest that has ever been proposed by sane men.

Mike had to fill the group in with his favorite snake story.

"My friend Bill has a cabin on a little lagoon down in the Jungas (mountain jungle) off the Rio Isabella. To get there you drive up over the cumbre toward Colomi and continue on toward Via Tunari, a trip of about fifty miles. You have to drive it on odd days as it is a one way road with no pass outs. In some places you can see the man made rock walls over hanging the road that the Chaco War prisoners built many years ago. These are spectacular as there is nothing but clouds below them for possibly 500 feet. These are along the ridge that eventually leads down below 14,000 feet. The road then winds down to pass under a waterfall that comes from four or five hundred feet above."

"The village of Via Tunari is a step back in time. The wooden buildings on either side of the road all lean in at least four directions with no visible means of support. The one and only motel is comprised of two 8'x16' concrete block wall buildings of two rooms divided by a concrete block wall in the center. This building has a thatch roof and two openings to either side of the central dividing wall. The restaurant is a 2'-0" block wall decorated with tile. The thatched roof is supported by six 4"x4" posts. The menu is varied as long as you like rice and beans."

"The road leads to a suspension float that crosses the Rio Isabella," Mike continued with more of the story.

"The suspension float is a relic of World War II. The United States was getting raw latex from the Brazilian jungle, and shipping it down the Amazon and on up into the U.S. The problem was that most of the latex was ending up on the floor of the Atlantic Ocean, courtesy of the German submarines."

"The U.S., in desperate need of the latex, sent the U.S. Army Corps of Engineers to Bolivia to build an access road into Brazil to transport the latex out to the Pacific. One of the obstacles was the Rio Isabella at Via Tunari. This problem was rather soon resolved by constructing towers on each side of the river and hanging cables from an anchorage on each side of the river and up over the towers. Structural steel was being used to build tanks and guns so the next best thing was to hang a suspended movable float on the cables. The float was moved from one side of the river to the other by a system of pulleys and cables that were hauled by a little six cylinder industrial gasoline engine. The float only had to be moved one hundred feet from one side to the other. The capacity of the float was two each 2 ½ ton trucks loaded with latex on the outward trip."

"If for some reason the winch engine stopped, then all the occupants of the float had to do was to uncoil the knotted rope on the float and drop down to a banana boat moving down stream at close to twenty miles an hour. The banana boats were about three feet wide by thirty feet long. This system still exists."

Mike went on explaining his plan.

"We would drive by Via Tunari, cross the bridge and drive on for another 30 miles to the lagoon. We would then paddle a small boat across the lake to Bill's cabin."

"The problem was that a month ago Bill was out in his dugout canoe fishing when a large swell overturned the canoe. Both he and his dog went into the water. The dog never made it to shore. There is an island in the middle of the lake that covers about two acres. Bill claims that an Anaconda about forty feet long lives on the island. His plan was to bait the island with a pig. As soon as the pig disappeared, he would re-bait the island with a second pig and build a picket fence around the island, with openings that the snake with a pig inside would not be able to pass through."

"That would be the signal to go there and shoot the snake with a tranquillizer so it could be towed out of the lake for a day, placed in the back of the Land Cruiser and driven for two days with a forty foot long snake in the back. How much tranquillizer would it take?"

For some reason Mike did not find any volunteers that wanted to tangle with a snake that size.

The dinner was very successful as everyone had a good chuckle out of that snake story, and the aborted plans of Bob and Mike to go to Jatun Rumi.

Mike went on to tell us of his tin mine near Oruro. The mine office and change house is at the bottom of a very steep mountain side. The miners live and eat at the base. If they were to climb up and down the slope they would take the full day. Mike had an inclined railway installed that ran from the base to the bench on the same level as the mine. A small gasoline hoist pulled the man car up and lowered it back down every day.

An Andean Condor lived on the top of the mountain, and did most of his feeding in the valley at the base camp level. This particular condor had at least a twelve foot wingspan. He would take off from his perch and glide around looking for food. He usually swooped down on an unsuspecting sheep or llama and knocked it off the side of the mountain. The condor would glide down to feed on the carcass. In its gluttony it found that getting back to the top of the mountain was more than it could handle. This wise old bird had solved that problem by hitching a ride on the man car. At first it would allow the miners to get into the man car to go to work, but it soon became very possessive and required the man car to be pulled up the slope with it as the only passenger. This soon became a ritual that the condor controlled.

CHAPTER 35

After a snake story and a condor story the rest of the crowd felt that they had little left to add. The party broke up shortly and Al escorted Carrie home. They were still laughing about Mike's wild stories. They settled down for an evening together and drinking some of Carrie's excellent coffee.

"Al, have you ever been to LaPaz and the ruins at Tiwanacu?" Carrie asked.

Al answered her, "No, but I did fly over the lake, and landed at the LaPaz airport."

"They are both must-see items for someone visiting Bolivia. You should plan to fly to LaPaz just to explore the old ruins and to walk the streets of one of the highest capitals of the world. Actually there is another capital city in Bolivia that is at about the same altitude. Sucre is the judicial capital while LaPaz is the administrative capital, both on the Altiplano. I have an idea. Why don't we fly up to LaPaz next Friday evening and spend the weekend there exploring the area?"

Blushing as she said it, "Don't take me wrong. This will be just a sight seeing trip, OK?"

Al thought about the possibilities of a trip such as that for about ten seconds and said, "Yes. I think that would be wonderful. It would be exceptional to have a local guide that knew the country and spoke the language, and was not looking for a very large tip. If you don't mind I'll pay the air fares, food and lodging if you will make the arrangements. You'll have all week to get everything organized. Just for your information, I haven't felt this close to anyone since I got out of the Army in 1953."

Carrie listened closely to what he'd just said. She hesitated for a moment, and then spoke quietly.

"I'll also confess that you're the first man I've wanted to keep company with since the death of my husband. Thank you very much for everything," she said in a trembling voice, which said much more than her words did.

"I think I'd better leave now for the hotel before I do something we both might not want at this time. Thank you for tonight. And thanks for being just you," Al said in a low voice.

Al called a taxi and regretfully left for the hotel, wondering if he had made a mistake.

CHAPTER 36

Friday morning arrived at last. Al met Severeno and the jeep outside of the hotel. They arrived at camp in time for breakfast and their early morning chat.

"We advanced another twenty four feet yesterday with four feet to go," reported Jesus. "Hopefully we can start clearing the main tunnel in front of the TBM next Monday."

The clearing of the trailing floor was going very well as were the repairs.

The initial pioneering of the access road had started using a Caterpillar D-6 dozer. This work was slow and quite dangerous as the operator had to keep a horizontal surface to work from or he could slide off the mountain into the canyon. They didn't need to lose any people or equipment. The pioneer crew had opened up about a mile of access trail.

Al and Severeno left the job and started down the hill until they met a 2½ ton flatbed piled high with steel ribs. The truck was broken down with the rear axle missing (actually about ten feet behind the truck). Truck drive train parts were strewn up the road for about fifty feet. They went back to the office to arrange for another truck and a crane to transfer the load from the disabled truck to the replacement truck. The contract hauler would be in that spot for a week or so or until he got the needed parts to put his truck back together. Such was life in the Andes.

They arrived at the hotel about an hour late, so his date with Carrie was late. This left them with a late movie time. Al called her from the hotel and explained the tardiness. She did not act very disturbed, taking it as a part of living in Bolivia. They decided to opt out for a nice dinner and a second showing of the movie. She was accustomed to the lack of hustling to do everything in Bolivia. Al was not, and was not sure that he would ever understand the minds of people who did. Al was all hurry up, go, go, and don't procrastinate. There was a schedule for everything that must be kept at all costs.

She slowed Al down to take life as it is. This was for now, anyway.

They found a very good Italian restaurant where excellent Veal Marsala or Veal Parmesan was on the menu as well as Oso Bucco. They decided on the Veal Marsala with an Italian tossed salad and a bottle of Chianti. They topped this off with some excellent flan.

By the time they had finished dinner it was well past the second movie showing, so they walked around the square, and then started along the Prado. There was a little bar and night club on the Prado, so they decided that as this was Friday evening and the night was young, they should treat themselves to a bit of entertainment. The entertainment was a very good piano player and a sultry singer belting out South American ballads. Even though their schedule was not as they had originally planned, they had a very wonderful time just living for the moment. They strolled up the street to Carrie's house where Al was invited in for a nightcap. She certainly knew how to brew a very good cup of coffee. Al finally left her house in the wee hours of the morning. They had discussed and partially settled most of the world's problems. She was one of the best conversationalists Al had ever known. During the course of their talks, Al admitted that he had not been entirely truthful when she had asked him if he were married.

"Carrie, you asked the other night if I were married, and I told you no. Actually, I was married to a young lady that I grew up with in Northern Vermont. We were married when I was in the army before leaving for Korea in 1951. I arrived back in the states in 1953 and was being discharged from the army at Fort Benning, Georgia when she drove to pick me up at the post. She was driving and was broadsided by a drunk driver. She was killed instantly. The police finally found me in a holding detachment on the army post. I seem to remember getting and staying drunk for a month."

"I drifted to California and took a job as a tunnel laborer. That job didn't last too long as it was found out that I was a veteran and had a degree in engineering. You might say that I was over qualified as a miner (I could read and write). I was almost immediately drafted as a shift engineer. The rest is history. That may explain why I am unattached and have been wary of getting too close to anyone. Work has been my way of dealing with the past," he explained to Carrie.

Al omitted the fact that he had not actually been discharged but rather had been put on standby reserve with the OSS, and later transferred to the new Special Forces Delta detachment and later the CIA. He could take whatever job he wanted, but would be on call for special projects as needed.

"I am so sorry that you've had that kind of memory and hope that you're getting away from it. I would like to be the one who helps you move on," Carrie commiserated with him.

They talked on for several more hours than they had planned. Each was finding the other one so easy to be with. It was more than just physical attractive. It was as if each had found a real soul mate.

"I'll be by about six o'clock so that we can have a day together to wander Cochabamba and the surrounding area," Al said as he left to go to the taxi.

CHAPTER 37

Tuesday morning arrived without fanfare. Al rolled out of bed and made himself ready for the day ahead. Al survived Severeno's driving without a cup of coffee. Once at the jobsite, he lurched into the mess hall for coffee and breakfast. Bob was waiting for him, as was Jesus.

"Now the crew will be opening up some of the main tunnel to launch the TBM. Before they do that we will drill fifty feet ahead and grout the rock to help support the fractured rock and to cut off any water inflows," reported Jesus.

"The access road pioneering has advanced about a mile. This allowed the crews to start grading the final alignment. The heavy highway equipment will be here today and tomorrow, so they can be put to work by the end of the week. Looks like things are shaping up," noted Bob. "The people from the states should be arriving in the next week."

Jesus commented, "We had a burro walk into the tunnel Saturday night. It scared the hell out of the miners because all that they could see at first was the shaggy grey shadow wandering up the tunnel. They could not make out what it was and thought that it was the ghost of one of the miner's dead father. They really spooked when the burro started to bray. The sound echoed off the tunnel ribs and really made a racket. The burro finally walked up close enough that they could see what it was. The problem then was that they were getting ready to blast and they couldn't get that stubborn animal to budge. It managed to kick a couple of the miners who were trying to be good Samaritans. It took them nearly 20 minutes to get the burro out of the tunnel. They were about ready to leave it there to see what the blast would do. The mess hall came close to having burro steak."

"Never a dull moment," commented Bob.

The rest of the day was taken up reviewing the claim and plans for the next few weeks. They did the paper work and late in the afternoon left for town.

Al called Carrie when he arrived at his hotel asking if she would like to go out for an Italian dinner.

Carrie said she thought that would be nice and that she would pick him up at the hotel in one half hour. They went to the same Italian restaurant that they had gone to last week. They opted for spaghetti and meat balls and a salad, all washed down by Chianti. Spumoni was their choice for dessert accompanied by espresso coffee. They discussed their upcoming trip to LaPaz and Tiwanacu. They were like two high school kids making plans for their first prom. They left the restaurant and headed for Carrie's house. They sat together on the sofa and made small talk reflecting on their mutual feelings for each other. Their snuggling became quite impassioned to the level that they both thought it would be better if they called it an evening. It was becoming obvious to both of them that they were becoming very serious about each other, possibly more so than either of them wanted at that time. Al left for the hotel before they both completely lost all reason.

It was another very enjoyable evening. He arrived at his hotel rather late and was once more faced with the prospect of the reluctant elevator. He was beginning to think that the elevator lurked in the dark reaches of its walled in chamber, just waiting for him to come along. It always groaned and rattled anytime he pushed the call button. The moment he boarded the monstrosity it would stall and bump its way to his floor. He was always thankful that he was able to get out and into his room without mishap.

Al was still very disturbed over his attachment for Carrie. These feelings had been put behind him for sixteen years as being something that was a hindrance to his lifestyle and work. He had avoided attachments for the same reasons that he had kept his head down in Korea. He was afraid of the consequences of having any feelings for anyone lest he lose them again. The pain of loss might be more than he could handle. Here was a very desirable woman that obviously had as deep an attachment for him as he had for her, but could he take the chance of hurting her or her hurting him? There were times lately when he found that he missed her very much when they were not together. He looked forward to talking to her and holding her in his arms. What to do now?

CHAPTER 38

"Ah! Another day at the mine," thought Al as he rode up the mountain with Severeno at the wheel. "This is another great day, no crazy truck drivers trying to run us off the road, no bus careening over the side of the mountain."

The temporary Master Mechanic, Ozzie Chippendale, arrived on site, accompanied by the temporary Tunnel Superintendent, Toni Parsonopolis, and an expert TBM driver, Hans Gerber, that afternoon. They were driven to the office and were briefed as to the immediate problems. They went into the tunnel to see for themselves what they would be up against. Ozzie climbed around the TBM, inspecting the machine and the trailing platform. He was accompanied by Hans who would be responsible for the training of three machine drivers. Toni went on into the access tunnel and the launching chamber ahead of the TBM to see what the grouting was accomplishing. The water inflow had been reduced from around 3000 gallons per minute to close to 500 gallons per minute. They all came out of the tunnel and back to the office with satisfied looks on their faces.

"All three of you will be assigned a car and a driver that will be at your side when you want them. I hope you realize that you may be here a little longer than you were told as we must make sure that the people here are trained and can operate on their own," Bob pointed out to them. They had pretty well assumed that that would be the case.

Bob then rounded up Jesus Domingo, the tunnel superintendent, and explained Toni Parsonopolis's assignment and that Toni was not there to replace him, but rather to be his mentor and to help him learn more about the TBM. This was well received by Jesus.

Bob found George Padilla, the Master Mechanic, and told him that Ozzie Chippendale would be on hand to teach him as much as possible about the maintenance of the TBM. He was not a replacement for George.

Pedro Vargas was called into the office and informed that Hans Gerber was an expert TBM operator and that Hans would teach Pedro and two operators about the TBM and how it operated until he knew they were experts.

All three men seemed relieved that they were not being replaced but rather that they were to be taught more skills that could be very valuable to them.

"It seems that that went over quite well without ruffling too many feathers," Bob said after the office was cleared of both the new and the old people.

"Why don't you call Carrie this evening and the two of you come on by the house for a few drinks and dinner?" Bob asked.

"I'll see if Carrie can make it tonight," Al said.

Al called Carrie as soon as he got to his room at the hotel and asked, "Are you free to go to the Adams around seven for dinner and drinks?"

"I was planning on the dinner as Agnes called me this morning and suggested it," Carrie said.

"Looks like I have been blindsided by plotting women once again. Why do I have the feeling that they are up to no good?" thought Al. "There have been times lately when I've felt that I was being manipulated by these gals. I must admit that it's a nice feeling having someone wanting to look after me."

They arrived at the Adams home in time for a drink before dinner, accompanied by some banter about Carrie and Al going to LaPaz unescorted. She blushed, and Al pled innocence to everything. He'd told Bob that he was going to LaPaz Friday afternoon and would be back Sunday evening.

Al and Carrie said their good byes and caught a taxi to Carrie's home.

Al stopped at Carrie's place on the way to the hotel to see if he needed to do anything about their trip to LaPaz. Being a very organized person, Carrie had everything well in hand.

"Al, would you like coffee and cake for an evening snack or would you prefer to walk down the street to the café and have a sultana and a beer?" The beer won out.

After Al left, Carrie sat and thought about her attachment for Al.

*

I wonder if I am being even a little intelligent becoming involved with Al. I've lived for a dozen years without being entangled with a man. I realize that I am envious of some of the women I know who have good husbands and a family. I have a respected position in the community and I have no financial worries.

However, there's something missing in my life. Is it the need to be involved with a man? What do I really know about Al? His past seems to be a big question mark. He's told me a lot about himself, but there always seems to be something else that he leaves unsaid. It seems that he's always on the move, never in the same place for a very long time. I keep getting the feeling that he leads a very dangerous life. I guess my problem is if I can live with the uncertainty of his way of life. If I commit myself to Al any more than I have so far, could I survive if something happens to him on one of his trips? What do I do if and when I know the truth of what he really does?

CHAPTER 39

There was a significant pall of smoke in the air as Al and Severeno drove toward the job on Wednesday morning. Al could see smudges of smoke over the sides of the mountain. Severeno explained that at this time of year the campesinos burn all the brush in the hope of a better crop of grass for their sheep and llama. This practice also helped feed the very few cattle herded by the campesinos.

The launching chamber was fully excavated and a concrete skid pad was being placed in the invert so that the TBM could be moved forward until the side grippers would be effective.

George Padilla was busy working with Ozzie Chippendale looking over his shoulder and handing out bits of knowledge about TBM maintenance and specific parts of the machine likely to give problems. They worked with the cutter specialist from the machine manufacturer setting up cutter repair schedules.

Hans Gerber had taken Pedro Vargas and two other hopeful TBM drivers under his watchful eye in the attempt to train them how to operate the machine and not turn it into a pile of scrap metal. He seemed to be making some headway, but no one would know until the machine started to advance.

Toni Parsonopolis was working with Jesus Domingo on what to expect from the machine and when to shut it down for maintenance.

Envero Aguilar was being briefed on what supplies had to be handled and brought into the tunnel in a timely fashion.

Locomotives and flat cars were made ready for use when for the TBM restarted. The road gang seemed to be reasonably self sufficient and were making reasonable progress.

The weekly progress meeting with Canadian Engineering was held amidst the usual obnoxious comments by Francois LaBatt. Not withstanding the fact that he had never seen a TBM before this project, he provided volumes of ridiculous details as to how it should be operated and maintained. All of this was useless information that he had gleaned from the local bars in Montreal. Even Pierre Lamont was fed up with his ranting and told him in so many words to either shut up or leave the meeting. This seemed to roll on past LaBatt. He just sat back and glared at everyone in the meeting.

The meeting closed out the day.

The next morning found that everything was as they had been left on Thursday. The plan was to allow the skid pad to set up until next Monday. The machine would then be moved forward into position against the new tunnel face. The new access road continued to be pushed toward the north end of the tunnel.

Bob was holding court with Toni, Ozzie and Jesus when Al walked in the door. They all seemed calm and relaxed so Al felt that every thing must be going smoothly. The four of them, all old friends, saw Al and started smirking.

"What's with all the smiles? Do you guys know something that I don't?" Al growled.

Bob replied, "We are just wishing we could take off from the job long enough to get a beautiful young lady to guide us around LaPaz and Tiwanacu."

That remark brought belly laughs from the group.

Severeno drove Al back to Cochabamba and his hotel. He once more took his chances with the hotel elevator, hoping that it would not quit half way between floors. The elevator performed on cue. It screamed and groaned, bumped and stumbled on its trip to the third floor.

CHAPTER 40

Al went to his room and packed his overnight bag for the weekender in LaPaz. Carrie came by to pick him up on the way to the airport for the noon flight to LaPaz.

The flight in the DC-7 was as comfortable as one would expect when flying over deep canyons and sliding alongside vertical walls of rock. It was difficult to tell which was worse, the down drafts or the updrafts. There was an ample number of each. The plane landed at El Alto Airport with neither Al nor Carrie being air sick. They walked through to pick up their meager luggage then went to the car rental kiosk for a car that had been reserved for them.

Carrie drove away from the airport, down the steep winding road into the city of LaPaz. They passed the barrio on the side hills. These consisted of stone or mud block huts with corrugated metal roofs and slop trenches for sanitation. The city streets were four lanes wide with granite buildings within ten feet of the curb. The Hotel Sucre was an old colonial structure, as were all the others along Calle Columbia. The city of LaPaz was a return to years long gone. The majority of the buildings were of granite of the colonial design that prevailed throughout the entire city.

The Hotel Sucre lived up to the colonial period with high ceilings, ornate woodwork, and more than ample space. The rooms were large and airy with antique beds and furnishing. Al and Carrie were fortunate to get two adjoining rooms. They went to their rooms and left their luggage. They opened the door connecting the rooms then went down to the hotel restaurant.

The food was better than most Bolivian food. They ordered steak and baked potatoes along with a salad and topped off with flan. They had a glass of fine red Argentine wine from Cordova with their meal. The coffee was the usual strong Bolivian brew.

They listened to the music in the lounge for about half an hour, and then decided that they should call it a day. Tomorrow would be a busy day. They kissed each other a very impassioned good night and separated to their own rooms.

Al had just started to doze when he was awakened by the presence of Carrie in his room. He cracked his eyes, just enough to watch her watching him. He kept his breathing slow and steady. She stood there for what seemed to be hours, but in fact was only minutes. She reached out her hand towards him, sighed, then turned and went back into her room. Al almost called out to her, but sensed that she, too, was working through new feelings just as he was. He had a hard time getting back to sleep.

"I hope you slept well last night," Carrie said as she came through the door at seven. "I slept the best that I have in years, just knowing that you were next door."

They had chorizos and scrambled eggs washed down with coffee for breakfast.

The rental car was found in the hotel garage. It was loaded with their gear and made ready to tour up on the Altiplano, headed for Tiwanacu. The road was of semi-graded gravel that produced untold quantities of dust. A rooster tail of dust followed them all the way across the flat expanse of the dry desert. The first thing that they saw was the hill projecting up out of the flat plain.

"This is the Piramide de Akapana, or Pyramid of Akapana," Carrie explained, "and was probably a religious temple. That is the Templete Semisubterrano, better known as the Partly Underground Temple with multitudes of stone heads. The very large open air temple is Kalasaya. The most famous is that structure over there, "the Puerta de Sol or the Sun Gate. Now that big statue is Pachamama or possibly the chief god. The smaller one is Inti, the Sun God."

Carrie went on to tell Al that a water supply line came down from a small reservoir on the top of the hill.

"The supply line is constructed of carved rhyolite blocks that dovetail to form a watertight box shaped pipe. The rhyolite came from those mountains fifteen miles away. A number of the blocks in these structures weigh more than one-hundred-thirty tons. The rhyolite is so hard that the Puerta de Sol shows very little weathering both above and below ground," Carrie explained. "The Tiwanacu Empire lasted from 2500 BC to 1172 AD before it disappeared."

"The farmers here managed some of the most extensive water supply systems known in the history of man. They were able to feed some eight million people." Carrie pointed out. "That is more than the present population of Bolivia."

Al was amazed at the structures and the problems of moving one hundred thirty ton stones fifteen miles.

"We've heard all our lives about the Egyptians and Babylonians and their cultures, but have never been educated as to the accomplishments of these people. Why?" Al questioned.

"Wait until you see some of the irrigation canals and water control structures they had. That will amaze you as an engineer," Carrie said.

They walked around the site of the ruins for about four hours, admiring the stone work and the carvings.

They drove to Lago Titacaca and watched the balsas (Indian reed boats) moving around on the surface of the lake. A dozen of them were pulled up on the shore so that Al and Carrie were able to make a close look at them.

Al said, "Those boats look just like the one of Thor Hyerdahl's Kon Tiki that he tried to cross the Pacific in. They also resemble the ancient Egyptian river boats. There doesn't seem to be much new in the world. We seem to have a lot of repetition down through the ages."

They watched the Indians fishing in the lake, but didn't see them catch anything. They decided to go back to LaPaz to look around there a bit.

Carrie drove back down the mountainous hills to the center of LaPaz. They went into the archeological museum. This was the best showing of ancient Inca artifacts that Al had ever seen. There were fully healed trepanned skulls with displays of various surgical tools that dated back several thousand years. There were several mummies as well as a multitude of fired clay pottery from ancient societies.

They wandered for three hours in the museum before leaving for the Hotel Sucre for dinner.

Before they left, Al bought Carrie a wide brimmed straw had with a red bow tied around the top of the hat. The bow had images of Inti and the Puerto de Sol knitted into it.

They had a great seafood (recently flown in) dinner and Chilean wine from the lake region of Chile, and Bolivian coffee freshly brewed.

After dinner they moved into the lounge to listen to the local musicians playing Amari and Quechua music.

The high altitude, the excellent meal, and drinks caused them to call it a day and head for their room. They kissed good night and went to their rooms to immediately fall into deep slumber.

It was 8:00 AM before they finally roused themselves for breakfast in the hotel dining room. Al was the first to arrive for breakfast, so ordered a large pot of coffee. He sat and sipped on the coffee until Carrie arrived a half hour later. They decided after a meal of ham and eggs to drive to the very bottom of the city to an area called "The Valley of the Moon." This was an amazing display of the end result of erosion. The scenery was made up of many pillars of clay and rock as well as strangely formed ridges that had been eroded over centuries, most probably by wind.

They then left to go back to the hotel for lunch and to check out, as they had a plane to catch for the flight back to Cochabamba.

The return fight was no more comfortable than had been the flight to LaPaz. They encountered the same updrafts and downdrafts and wild swings around mountain side walls. The plane finally landed at Cochabamba after about three bounces on the tarmac.

It was getting to be quite late so Carrie picked up her Land Cruiser and dropped Al off at his hotel then went on to her house.

Al couldn't help but think that this was an amazing weekend, but more than that, he had met perhaps the most incredible woman of his life. For the first time, he realized that he might have to find some way to make room for something else in his life, other than work and more work, excitement and intrigue.

CHAPTER 41

Severeno appeared as if by magic as Al walked out the door of the hotel.

"How was your trip to LaPaz? Did you go to Tiwanacu? That is a most wonderful place, especially for Bolivianos," quizzed Severeno.

"The trip was very nice, and we enjoyed Tiwanacu and LaPaz," answered Al.

As usual, Bob was holding down a table in the mess hall with Ozzie, and Jesus. Al joined them for coffee and breakfast.

"Tell us all about your guided weekend on the Altiplano. Did you see everything that you wanted or did you miss anything?" asked Bob.

"We had a great time and saw most of the area," rejoined Al. "Have you started the TBM yet? Is it being moved forward?"

"Hopefully we will have it pushed to the rock face by the end of day shift. We will only work day shift today and will start swing shift tomorrow and then go to the third shift on Wednesday. That way every operator and crew will have worked one complete shift under supervision of our temporary people. Thursday and Friday should start the ball rolling on production. Saturdays will be maintenance, cutter changes and whatever else is needed," Bob answered very enthusiastically.

"The access road is starting to open up to about a mile a day of pioneering and about a quarter mile a day of road bed grading and shaping," said Jesus.

They finished breakfast and decided that they should get some fresh air by driving the access road that had been pioneered to date.. There was no hindrance of trees as there was nothing but light brush on the slopes along the alignment. They drove around a curve and saw LaBatt standing by his Jeep. He waved to them as they drove by.

They had just rounded the next curve when Al yelled, "Stop! I don't hear the compressors or the drills, do you? Quick back up. Lets get to hell out of here. I think they are about ready to blast that overhanging ledge down there."

They had just returned to the shelter of the large rock knob at the curve when the explosion shook the ground, and sent rocks flying by them.

"Wow! That was close, Now why didn't LaBatt tell us they were about to shoot that ledge? We could have been buried under the rock fall. Let's find LaBatt and find out what is going on."

They drove back to where they had seen LaBatt, but he had left. They inquired about him when they returned to camp. They were told that he had returned and left camp in a big hurry.

Satisfied that those things were going well on the road, they went to the tunnel portal and walked into the trailing floor of the machine. The forward movement could be felt as the TBM was jacked ahead by the grippers pushing against the rock walls.

Wednesday morning the machine was once more started and began cutting the rock in the face. The cutter head was turning at about 3.0 revolutions per minute, and ground up rock had started to come off the conveyor in a steady stream. This was truly a sight to be seen, especially after it had been shut down for over two months.

Al had dinner at Carrie's home in celebration of the machine startup. He started to commit himself a half dozen times but stopped when he lost his nerve. He thought, "Here I am, the fearless undercover operator scared out of my mind to commit to the most wonderful woman I have ever known. Is it that I am afraid to possibly hurt her when she eventually learns what I really do?"

They commiserated with one another between kisses until he felt that he had to leave for the hotel or ask to stay over. He finally left for the hotel at a late hour.

Thursday morning the machine once again started chewing up the rock in the face of the tunnel. Yesterday the face was advanced a total of 30 feet in one shift.

He was ecstatic the machine was working well, so took Carrie out for a Chinese dinner. He finally excused himself around one in the morning to return to the hotel.

Friday morning found the machine had moved 90 feet in three shifts. Al was told that it was expected that it should be the minimum advance from now on.

Al reported, "The machine is doing all that it is required to do, so now I could with a clear conscience, take a few days off to sightsee with you if you would like to."

CHAPTER 42

Al went back to the job on Saturday and was told that they had advanced another 90 feet. That meant a total of 270 feet for the first partial week.

The crew was on maintenance mode today.

"The road crew has pioneered two and a half miles while the road bed shaping has moved one and one quarter miles this week. Not bad for amateurs," said Bob. "Looks like you are close to being wound up here, doesn't it, Al?"

"Yes, you're right, but I think I'll hang around on your payroll for a couple of more weeks just to be able to look over your shoulder and nag you. Besides, I haven't had a good vacation in a long time, and guess who I intend to vacation with? Besides, I've been invited to another party tonight. Do you mind if I borrow the Jeep without Severeno for a week or two?" Al asked, quite innocently.

Al went back to town with Severeno, and then commandeered the jeep. As soon as he hit town, he called Carrie to see what her plans were for the next two weeks. He knew that he wouldn't be able to keep away from the job for two weeks, but the plan sounded good. Carrie declared, "I would be delighted to drive us out to the Incayacta ruins on Sunday."

Carrie said that she would like to show him a really interesting Inca site that was only fifty miles from Cochabamba. They could go there Sunday, spend the day and take along a picnic lunch.

They drove to The Suarez residence for the Saturday evening party.

They arrived appropriately a half hour late and were met by Maggie at the door.

The same crowd was there, including Major Ward and Major Wolf.

Major Wolf sauntered by and in a relatively low voice told Al that he would like to meet with him Monday morning, as there was something that he must bring to his attention. He said he would come over to the hotel bar at eight. He then walked off.

The proverbial bad ass actor, Francois LaBatt, was in attendance, making a nuisance of himself with any woman that happened near him.

Al walked over to him and asked" Why did you let us drive by on the access road when you knew they were going to blast? Were you trying to get us killed?"

LaBatt grinned and turned to leave. Al grabbed his shoulder but was wrenched away from him by Bob who laughingly suggested that he didn't want Al put in a Bolivian jail for killing LaBatt.

Mike Whitman made an appearance with a very nice looking young lady that he would later marry, provided she could keep him home from hunting and fishing long enough for the ceremony.

Mike asked if Al and Carrie would like to shoot some pigeons at Mike's finca about 20 miles east of San Pablo on Sunday afternoon.

Al said, "We had other plans for Sunday afternoon, but would really like a rain check."

Mike said, "We can make it during the week if you can get away from the job for a day."

They agreed to let him know which day would be the best.

Jaimie Perez, the local chief of police, was on hand to sample the wine and to catch up on the local gossip.

Will Barret, the Project Engineer and his wife, made the rounds at the party and greeted everyone they knew. George Thomas, the American Consul in Cochabamba, was there, and even the Canadian contingent arrived about an hour late, in keeping with local custom.

The party stayed relatively sober and no one became complete bores by annoying everyone else.

Carrie and Al left by about midnight. She dropped him at the hotel saying that she would be by around ten the next morning to pick him up for the picnic at Incayacta.

CHAPTER 43

Carrie drove up in her bright red Toyota Land Cruiser promptly at ten, a trait that Al found very nice.

The Land Cruiser was loaded with a picnic basket and some Chilean wines that Carrie thought might come in handy, especially if it was at all cool on the site of Incayacta (Inca city).

They drove past Punata a distance of about fifty miles on a rough paved road. There were no signs to let them know where they were except for the military check station several miles out of Punata. The old ruins could be seen from the road. They made a right hand turn up a gravel road to the site. There was a small casa a few hundred yards to the left of the turn. Carrie parked the Toyota at the end of the road. They had to walk the last one hundred yards to the rim of a canyon that defined one side of Incayacta.

Carrie described the city to Al.

"Incayacta was thought to have been a military post. The city sits on a wedge of rock that is bound on its wide end by a large rock outcrop and on both sides by deep river canyons that provide natural protection from raiders. The canyons converge at the low end of the city. The populace lived outside the city proper. A major building in the center of the city appears to have been about 240 feet long by about 60 feet wide. This may have been a gathering place for the people of Incayacta. The roof was thought to have been forty feet high. There are evenly spaced indentations in the soil that suggest the locations of posts for supporting the roof structure. There are many other foundations of local rock walls filled with soil. Water was delivered by canals from a falls upstream of the city. Many smaller foundations suggesting housing for the officials are evident throughout the city."

Carrie explained to Al about the hidden caves just upstream of the wall.

"The priests had their sacrificial alters in some of the caves along the river. You must climb down to the river level by way of that little goat trail over there and then follow the river back up about a hundred yards to the second little four foot opening in the rock face. Crawl inside and you would find a very comfortable cavern with water and a collection of grass for bedding. If I ever found that I had to hide from anyone that's where I would go. The caves can be reached from the other side of the river by a very narrow trail starting at the falls."

Al and Carrie sat near one of the major walls with their picnic basket and wine. They spread a blanket on a large flat rock and set it as a table.

"You know, this is a major world wonder. Anyone building structures like the community hall had to have a very good understanding of structural engineering. This at a time in world history when Europeans were having difficulty with simple water supplies, let alone major structures," Al told Carrie.

"If you think this is something, maybe we should drive out tomorrow so you can see the Inca irrigation systems," Carrie said in her teacher's voice.

While they were sitting there eating, they were aware of a pair of black eyes peering at them from behind a rock wall nearby.

"Carrie, I don't think that we're alone out here. There seems to be a midget over there behind the wall. I think that he wants us to share our meal with him."

"Why don't we wait until we are through eating and are ready to leave? Then we can give him our left over food. If we give him some food right now, all his little buddies will raid us," Carrie said laughing.

After they had eaten and picked up all the leftovers, they motioned to the young boy who had been watching them. He was possibly eight years old, ragged and dirty. He told Al that for a small payment he would show them where the Incas had buried their gold. He was told that most probably if he knew where the Inca gold was buried there was no way he was about to tell a couple of gringos.

Feeling good about themselves and the world in general, they gave the boy all the food he could carry. When they arrived at the bottom of the hill near the casa, the boy was walking across the field. All the food had been ditched someplace.

Carrie and Al drove back to town, arriving in time to clean up for a dinner date. They decided to go to the Luna Bleu for Italian. Dinner was very musical with a roaming troubadour making the rounds playing his violin and singing romantic ballads. After a few glasses of Chianti, Carrie was starry eyed. They had spaghetti bolognaise, a salad and Italian bread. This was topped off by a generous portion of spumoni and a cup of coffee.

"Al, this has been another very wonderful day that I shall never forget. I keep thinking how nice it would be if we could just keep everything in a time warp and never let it fade away."

"Carrie, you're spoiling me so badly, I am not at all sure I want to leave you here by yourself. I don't look forward to leaving and returning to San Francisco. I haven't been this relaxed for many years," Al said in a rather husky voice.

They went back to Carrie's house for coffee and a good night kiss.

Al laughingly said, "I'd better leave soon or you might have to make me breakfast."

Carrie smiled and answered. "That might be a very nice idea."

CHAPTER 44

Al just made his meeting with Major Wolf at nine that morning, at the bar in the hotel.

"How did your weekend go, Al? Did you have an enjoyable time at the cocktail party and how did you find the scenery at Incayacta? Don't act shocked. We were just keeping track of you, so you wouldn't get into any more trouble," grinned Major Wolf.

"You seem to have a pretty good spy network. Do you also know when I went to the bathroom? You seem to know everything else. OK! What the hell is this sudden interest in my welfare all about?" growled Al.

"My leader in San Francisco had a long talk with your boss, John Christman. He told Christman only what he specifically had to know. Christman said that he had been planning to appoint you as South American Operations Manager, as the former one had resigned under duress. He said that you would be assigned to stay in South America for a period of not more than six months, or until a suitable replacement could be found so that he could get you back to San Francisco for better things."

Al listened, with an inquisitive look on his face.

"OK! When does the other shoe drop? What kind of games do you guys want me to play? Undercover hit man for the Mafia?" Al asked rather sarcastically.

Major Wolf smiled and answered, "None of the above will be needed. We just want you to keep track of the drug cartel leaders and various other bad guys' whereabouts and their movements around South America. Keep me informed and we'll take care of the rest. This means that you'll have to move around the country quite a lot without their knowing what you're up to. What you use for a cover is up to you. You're a good tourist and amateur archeologist, as well as an engineer. Have a good time on our buck."

"Is that all?" asked Al.

"That's about it. Just don't be surprised if you feel someone is covering your back," said Major Wolf. "See you later."

Al left the hotel bar, went to his room and called the job to tell Bob that he would be there shortly.

"Al, you sly old fox. Why didn't you tell us that you were being assigned as South American Operations Manager? We'll be here to greet you with confetti or whatever we use to meet our new boss," laughed Bob.

"I didn't know until a few minutes ago myself. It wasn't on my schedule," said Al.

"I just got a message from San Francisco headquarters. Congratulations," Bob chuckled.

Al called Carrie to tell her that he had to go to the job for a while.

"Congratulations, Al. I'll be waiting for you," Carrie said.

"How the hell did you find out so soon? I just heard a few minutes ago, myself. I called Bob to tell him that I would be going up to the job for a while and he already knew. OK! He called Agnes and she called you. That's how you knew so soon. So much for secrets around here," said Al.

When Al arrived at the job site some smart ass had painted a large sign and stuck it on a post in front of the office.

PRIVATE PARKING - ALBERT PROVO ONLY

ALL OTHER VEHICLES WILL BE TOWED

Al waved to the smiling group of co-conspirators and told them that henceforth they should bow before him. They should all be presenting a bottle of good Scotch to him.

Bob gave him a copy of the wire from San Francisco in which John Christman told him of his appointment as South American Operations Manager.

After reading this, Al decided that he was going to take a couple of weeks back vacation time to find his way around the area. He then left and rode back down to town. He went directly to see Carrie at her house.

CHAPTER 45

Carrie was bubbling with joy at the news of Al's promotion, partly for Al and partly for the fact that he would be around Bolivia for a longer time.

"Al, are you still going to take a little time off? If you are, maybe we could go pigeon shooting with Mike at his finca?" Carrie suggested.

"Sounds good to me, I'll call Mike now and see when we can go. I don't have a shotgun though. Where can I find one for a few days?"

Carrie smiled and pointed, "See that walk-in safe over there? It's full of guns that my father left me. I think you might find the Purdys to your liking. If not, there're a few Daleys and even a Winchester or two. Take your pick."

"Carrie, you are just full of surprises. I suppose you yourself are a very good wing shot, also."

Al called Mike and the pigeon shoot was set for the next day. Mike said he would pick them up at seven the next morning, so that they could spend the day and maybe even do a little horseback riding.

Al suggested that they should pick out a shotgun and some ammunition for the pigeon shoot the next day.

"Is this one OK?" asked Carrie, as she handed Al an engraved Purdy side by side double 20 Gauge.

Al took one look at the Purdy and said, "This one looks too valuable to take out in the field. All that inlay and fancy engraving almost makes me afraid to shoot it. The rest of the shotguns are all of the same level of engraving and inlay with silver and gold. Your father was certainly a connoisseur of fine shotguns."

"He liked to bird hunt and taught me how to shoot birds here in Bolivia and in Texas. Take a closer look at the rest of the guns in that safe. You must be careful so that the guns won't get all rusty from your drooling all over them."

"I'm completely flabbergasted at all these valuable guns here in this house. Is this safe enough protection? Do the ruling politicos have any idea about these?" Al asked.

Carrie replied, "I'll take that matching 20 gauge Purdy for myself. Mike said that there are hundreds of pigeons that he wants to get rid of, so let's take six boxes of #9 shot. That should do it for the birds. Here, take this for kicks," Carrie said handing him a .45 Colt auto.

They got all their gear together and decided it was time to eat dinner at the Chinese restaurant. They drove there in Carrie's Toyota and were greeted by the proprietor as old friends. He suggested sweet and sour soup, fried pot stickers, mushi pork with plum sauce, Mongolian beef and shrimp fried rice, all with green tea.

Carrie thought that would be wonderful. They ate their meal with chop sticks and took the leftovers home in small paper boxes, just in case they were hungry later in the evening.

They arrived back at Carrie's house where they sat around and talked for several hours until it was suggested that Al should, for appearances, go back to his hotel and return in time for an early breakfast in the morning. Mike had said that he would be there at seven.

Carrie told Al not to pout just because he had to go back to his hotel early.

*

Mike showed up promptly at seven that next morning, with Lucio Esparenza. Lucio was an old hunting and fishing buddy of Mike's.

Mike drove out to his finca about 30 miles east of San Pablo. Actually it was 20 miles on a paved road and another 10 miles on a wash board gravel road to the finca. The main buildings were a house and a horse and cattle shed off some 100 yards from the house. The house was a one story plastered finish painted a dull yellow with blue trim at the doors and windows. The roof was red Spanish tile like most of the roofs on the better buildings around the area. A large veranda spread across the front of the house leaving a ten foot wide space to lay back in the shade during the few hot days that occurred here. There was no furniture in the house. The horse and cattle shed was a clone of the house, but did not have the veranda. It was fitted with wide doors to admit wagons and carriages.

The number of pigeons sitting on the roof peak and any place they could perch was unbelievable. There were close to three or four hundred birds flying around. It didn't take much imagination to understand Mike's desire to thin out the flocks. Mike and Lucio led Carrie and Al around to the end of the buildings and Mike instructed everyone to shoot as many birds as possible. It took nearly two hours to cull the flock down to close to fifty birds. Mike found some barrels and put the birds in the barrels for the campesinos. He explained that these birds were too tough to eat; however the campesinos would have a real feast on them.

They stopped the bird shoot to eat lunch when Mike said, "We'll have time to go for a ride on the horses. We can ride up to the foothills then back. That will be about fifteen miles round trip. It is a very picturesque ride."

They saddled four horses, one a palomino, one a Rhone, the third a black and white with a brown head and rump, and the fourth a white mare with black feet and mane. All the horses were mares, as they usually are easier to handle. Mike led the parade, Carrie and Al followed with Lucio taking the rear. The ride was through scrub and cactus over rocky soil that did not seem to be very hospitable to any other vegetation. They at last came to a struggling trickle of water that seemed to be losing out to the thirsty sandy creek bottom.

They stopped several times to drink from their canteens, but continued on after a very short rest. Some of them declined getting off their horses as they felt they probably would not be able to saddle up again. The party finally arrived at the half way point and after a rest stop climbed back on the horses for the return trip to the finca. The only wild life creatures they had seen were a few birds and rabbits. When they arrived back at the finca they found that all the barrels and birds were gone, hopefully as a meal for someone. The foursome arrived back in Cochabamba just before dark after a very exhilarating day in the great out of doors.

Carrie and Al thanked Mike and Luicio for a very fine day, then went in the house to clean the shotguns. Her father had taught her right. She knew what she was doing. They cleaned up and then went to the Italian restaurant for dinner.

Carrie sat at the table looking at Al and finally said, "I had a wonderful time today shooting and horseback riding with you. We seem to enjoy so many similar things. I hope that you can stay here in Cochabamba. I would like that very much."

Al replied, "I must make a living and to do that I have to go where I'm told. I can't think of anything better than to stay here in Cochabamba with you. It would be very wonderful to be able to see you every day. Sometime though, I must go to work, so let's just enjoy what we have for as long as we can."

"How would you like to go trout fishing at the Rio Secure with Mike and Lucio? Mike asked me if we would be interested, say this coming

Thursday and Friday. We are supposed to go to a cocktail party Saturday evening. Don't want to miss that, now do we?" Al asked.

"That sounds good to me. I like trout fishing. Bet I can catch a bigger one than you," said Carrie.

Carrie turned to Al and in a very serious tone asked, "Seeing that you may be doing a lot of traveling and will be away from Cochabamba for a few days at a time, what do you think about moving over here to my house? I have an extra bedroom with a separate bath that you could use. This would give you some place to store your personal belongings. You would have the comforts of home, a place to eat and relax. My maid would even do your laundry. How is that for an offer? There are no ties connected to this offer unless you want to make them."

Al stammered that it was a great offer, much more than he had ever hoped for. "The only problem may be local gossip. How would it look to the school board to have me under your roof?"

Carrie blushed and said, "I don't think it would create any more raised eyebrows than your being a late visitor here nearly every evening. Is it a deal?"

"When do I move in?" asked Al. "Would Friday be too soon?"

When Al got back to the hotel that night, he called Mike and set up the fishing trip for Thursday and Friday. Mike said that he would pick them up at seven that Thurday.

"We will be driving part way on the old Santa Cruz Highway. The turn off takes us onto a gravel road up over 14,000 feet altitude, then down into the mountain jungle at 7,000 feet. We will have to camp out in sleeping bags as there is no shelter other than trees."

CHAPTER 46

Al decided that he should make an appearance at the job site, at least for a couple of hours to find out how the TBM was working

Al had dressed and was heading to the job site when he recalled that he hadn't seen, nor heard from the convivial construction inspector for several days. He had not saluted them with a spray of rocks and pebbles as they drove down the hill. Al must remember to ask Bob if Pierre had sacked him and sent him back to Canada.

Half way through breakfast Al remarked, "I have not seen LaBatt for a few days, is he on vacation?"

He received a lot of stares that suggested that those people didn't know and couldn't care less about LaBatt.

"I am a bit worried about him; we haven't heard a word about him for two days. He left here in his company jeep Monday late in the evening before you guys returned from exploring the North Portal," said Pierre.

Mike picked them up at seven. As they drove along the road, Mike proceeded to recite a story about a previous fishing trip he had made to this location.

"A friend of Bob's, Peter, flew down from Boston just to go fishing. To say that he was a rabid trout fisherman would be an understatement. He brought his handmade Orvis bamboo rod. This was his pride and joy. We left Cochabamba and drove up over the pass, then down to the jungle river known as Rio Secure. We arrived there about noon and decided to start teasing the trout. Peter, Bob, and I went along the river to a place where we could get to the water. We started casting Mepps spinners and almost immediately had some good hits. Peter hooked a nice 18 inch German Brown that did not really care to be caught. The trout took off upstream into a jumble of brush that the locals used as fish traps. The fish swam into and around and over and then through the maze of brush. Peter lowered his rod and then we heard a pop, then several more pops as his rod started to pull apart at the joints. The fish was still making its escape upriver."

"Bob did the expedient thing. He jumped hip deep into the very cold water to head the fish off. Bob managed to get his hands on the trout and trap it. Then the problem was whether to cut the line or to thread the trout back through all that brush. This was settled as no one had extra fishing line so there were the three of us threading that trout back down stream."

"The next bit of ingenuity was shown when Peter hooked a 14 inch Rainbow trout. This trout had a different way to escape. The trout merely swam into a little cove the locals had made as a trap. As the fish was being landed on the little beach, it threw the hook. Bob decided that the trout was not going to get away that easily, so he grabbed it by the tail when it poked its head between some rocks. A tail hold on a slippery trout is not to be recommended, so Bob pulled out a pair of fishing pliers and grabbed the fish by the tail. He got the trout but also got soaked in the process.

"The sad part of the story was that Peter became very seriously ill from altitude sickness. His threw up everything except his toenails. Those were firmly attached. We loaded him into the jeep the next noon as he was almost comatose. We decided to get back to Cochabamba as soon as possible to get him to a source of oxygen at the hospital. We reached the top of the pass and he came out of it and felt reasonably well. I heard several months later that the shock of altitude sickness had caused him to lose all his body hair. The hair eventually grew back over the next year."

Both Carrie and Al promised Mike not to duplicate the effort of Peter and Bob and especially not to succumb to altitude sickness. They each caught three nice Rainbows and a German Brown that afternoon. They set up a lean-to tent and built a fire in front of it. They ate fresh fish for dinner, accompanied by bread and beans. Sleeping bags were the only means of staying warm as the temperature dropped about twenty degrees during the night.

Friday, the fishing was again great, but about noon time they were getting tired and decided to return to Cochabamba.

Carrie and Al both told Mike that this had been one of the best fishing trips they had ever been on. They had trouble expressing their gratitude for his taking them out.

Al again told Carrie that there would most likely be times when he would have to travel and be away from her for several weeks at a time. That was one of the problems with his work. He had to go where the work was.

Carrie did not want to hear about his leaving and said so in a great many words. She would not let him go to sleep that night. She said that he was the love of her life and that she wanted and needed him.

They talked about their enjoying the next week and where they would go so that they could be alone.

"We did say something about Mt. Tunari," she murmured.

CHAPTER 47

A week earlier, late on Monday afternoon, Isabella Vasquez returned to her casa with the sheep she had been herding on the mountain side. Isobella was eight years old, short with black braids and deep black round eyes that miss nothing. Her family chore was to herd the sheep every day to good grazing on the side hill grasses. She was very excited when she found her mother inside the casa.

"Mama, I was watching the sheep like I always do on the side of the mountain when I saw a big cloud of dust up near the cumbre. It looked like something had fallen off the side of the mountain. I was on the far side of the canyon."

Her mother said that they would tell the alcalde Saturday when they went to the market.

Pepito was digging potatoes with his mother and sisters on Monday afternoon when he saw a big cloud of dust on the other side of the valley. He told his mother about it, but she was too busy picking up the potatoes and putting them in her back pack. He forgot about the dust cloud because he was only six years old and was tired from picking up potatoes.

Thursday mornings were not normally busy for Jaimie Perez, the chief of police. He was very competent and very Prussian in his approach to his profession. He brooked no nonsense from his force of rather elite police who were concerned with criminal activities. He held the traffic police in contempt as being corrupt and sloppy in their work. He had been a Colonel in the German Army and still looked all spit and polish with razor sharp creases in his uniform. His mind was just as sharp as were the creases in his trousers.

It was a bit annoying to have an unwashed truck driver ushered into his neat office this early in the morning. After all, he had just started his first cup of coffee. The truck driver bowed and scrapped and blubbered all over himself in the face of such obvious authority. The Chief became impatient and at last asked him why he was bothering him.

"What do you want with me that you weren't able to tell my Sergeant at the front desk?"

"Jefe, I am but a poor truck driver and am afraid to cause trouble for El Jefe, but Monday when I was driving down the mountain on my way from the Beni I saw something that I feel you should know about. As you know, Monday we drive west and on Tuesday we drive east. I was afraid to come to you before, but my priest told me that I should report what I saw to you."

All the time the truck driver was massaging the rim of his hat in mortal fear.

"What is your name? What do you want to tell me that has you this upset?" asked the Chief.

"My name is Pedro Gonzales, Jefe. Monday morning I was hauling a load of cocoa leaf from over the Cumbre and was just starting down the mountain when I looked and saw a grey car coming up the road at a very high speed. We were on the top hairpin curve when I saw that it was a Jeep. He went by me on the curve so I am not sure what happened to him, but I think that he must have gone over the side of the road, because I saw a lot of dust blow out past the curve. I have driven past the same spot since then, but did not see anything."

"Thank you for bringing this to my attention. Please leave your name and how you may be contacted with the desk Sergeant," said the Chief. "I will send someone to look at the area."

After the truck driver left, the Chief of Police called in his desk Sergeant.

"Have you heard of anyone missing in the past few days? Have we had any other reports of accidents in the area of the Cumbre?"

"No, Jefe, we haven't had any missing persons reports, or any reports of accidents," answered the desk Sergeant.

Friday morning found Pierre Lamont of The Canadian Engineering Company walking briskly into the Police station.

"I would like to talk to Chief Perez as soon as possible. Is he in this morning?"

"I regret that he is not in the office this morning, but he should be here on Monday morning. Can I give him a message?" asked the Desk Sergeant.

"Just ask him if he has seen Senor LaBatt in the past few days. He knows Francois LaBatt as he has met him several times at parties. Thank you, Sergeant."

Pierre then left the police office thinking that he might encounter the Chief over the weekend at a party, but he was unable to meet with the Chief over the weekend as the Chief was in LaPaz on business.

CHAPTER 48

The Chief asked his Desk Sergeant early on Monday morning to drive up to the cumbre just to see if Pedro Gonzales had really seen a vehicle go over the edge of the road. It took just about an hour for the Desk Sergeant to arrive at the cumbre. He climbed out of the Jeep and walked about twenty feet along the edge to see tire marks indicating a vehicle of some kind had gone over the side. The road nearly overhung the slope below, so that the Sergeant had to stretch his body out over the edge rather precariously to see below.

He did see a jeep door with the Canadian Engineering logo lying about 100 feet below on a small ledge. Looking on down the slope, he could make out the remains of a Jeep. He could not be certain as to whether or not that he could see a body lying beneath the wreckage. It would be very foolhardy for him to attempt to climb down to the wreck without help. He decided to return to the police headquarters and advise the Chief as to his discovery.

He returned to the office at noon, just in time to catch the Chief. He told the Chief that he would need the services of the rescue team to get down to the wreck. A crane would be needed to extricate the wreck from below.

The Chief explained to him that a local alcalde had come by the office to advise him that a young girl had seen the vehicle go over the side of the mountain on the previous Monday.

"The Jeep and driver must be retrieved as the Project Resident Engineer Pierre Lamont had reported one of his men missing since last Monday. Get a crew out there as soon as possible and get the body in to the morgue. While you are about it, retrieve the Jeep and transport it down here to headquarters. You may have to engage a crane from Senor Adams at BOSCO to get the jeep out of there," instructed the Chief.

The Sergeant left with the rescue team at first light the next morning. He had contacted Bob Adams and arranged to meet the crane at the cumbre on Tuesday morning.

The rescue team surveyed the wreck site and decided on anchoring their ropes to their emergency truck. Their ropes were only 250 feet long, so they would have to rappel down and tie off before going down the rest of the way. Two of the men went down while the other four stayed above to do whatever they could to help. The two rappelled to a small ledge where they could tie off for the final decent. When they finally arrived at the wreck an hour latter, they did not see a body near or under the crumpled body of the Jeep. They then began a systematic search of the area, hanging off their rappel ropes.

After another hour of searching, one of the searchers noticed some bloody rags caught in the low brush downhill from the wreck. He continued searching in that general area and encountered a battered body lying in the brush. The body was barely recognizable because of the force of the impact and the fact that it had lain in the open for a week.

They called down a stretcher to use to remove the body. They tied the body onto the stretcher and helped guide it up the slope, sliding it around rocks and outcrops.

A rough terrain crane from BOSCO had arrived just as the body was pulled over the edge of the road. The Crane was positioned so that the cable from the crane could reach the Jeep. The rescue team then returned to the wreckage to secure the cable and to signal the crane operator to hoist the Jeep to the road.

The demolished Jeep was finally loaded on a flatbed truck for delivery to the police headquarters compound. The body was driven to the morgue.

Pierre Lamont arrived at the morgue where he was asked to identify the body. Pierre was much shaken, but when the morgue attendant uncovered the body he was able to state categorically that it was not Francois LaBatt.

His statement raised many questions from Chief Perez.

"If it is not LaBatt then, who is it and where is LaBatt? That was his assigned Jeep, was it not? How did this man die? Was it from the accident?"

Pierre said, "I think that it is George Jordan. George and Patricia have been staying at the Hotel Vista Tunari. I heard somewhere that they are Argentines or possibly Canadians."

Later in the afternoon, Dr. Lopez completed the autopsy and reported to Chief Perez that the John Doe had been shot by a small caliber bullet in the back of his head. It was done as though it was an assassination carried out by a gang.

Chief Perez had not been idle. He had been through the hotel room and found an Argentine passport for one George Jordan. The description and photo matched the corpse. Jordan had apparently claimed Canadian citizenship under a dual citizenship rule.

Patricia was not to be found. The luggage of both George and Patricia was still in the room. They had not checked out of the hotel. The desk clerk volunteered that he had seen Patricia leave with a dark haired gringo who had a rather large black mustache. She had seemed to be nervous about something.

Perez decided not to pass up the possibility that they had both been killed and her body had been disposed of somewhere en route to the accident scene, if it was an accident.

The Chief had the truck driver, Pedro Gonzales, brought in for further questioning.

"Pedro, did you see anything strange or unusual near the accident last week?" the Chief asked.

"No, Jefe, I saw nothing. I can ask my helper and some of the men that rode up with me if they saw anything if that will help".

CHAPTER 49

Bob and Al sat in Bob's office in complete disbelief that the man in the Jeep had been George Jordan rather than Francois LaBatt. They were both convinced that if anyone were targeted to die it would have been LaBatt.

"You know, Bob, I'm sort of curious as to what George and Patricia were doing here. Their stories never came out the same. They claimed to be Argentine citizens, but held dual citizenship. They said they went to Santa Cruz to visit friends but the friends were either non-existent or had run out on them. For George to have been in LaBatt's company Jeep causes me to wonder what their connection is or was.

Jamie Perez was considerate enough to inform Al that the story on the Jordan couple was a cover put out by the Canadian government to protect them on this assignment. The Canadian Embassy had been pushing a lot of buttons since learning of George Jordan's death and they were extremely concerned for Patricia.

Al had met the Jordans' in the hotel bar the day that he arrived in Cochabamba and they had told him that they were driving to Santa Cruz. George and Patricia Jordan, however, had left early the next morning on a local flight to LaPaz, Bolivia, hoping to meet their contact at the Canadian Embassy. They found their contact and were given final instructions regarding the arrest.

They acquired .22 caliber pistols and a Fairburn commando knife, both of which would be easily carried aboard their flight back to Cochabamba. They also acquired a scoped hunting rifle in .270 caliber. They now had a safe-house when the time arrived that required them to disappear for a while with their prisoner.

Saturday found them back in Cochabamba at the standup cocktail party at the U.S. consulate. They were recognized by the American that they had met the day they arrived. They also glimpsed their target for a few seconds. They felt that there was no need to hurry as time and stealth were on their side. They would bide their time until things were right.

LaBatt was sitting at the corner table at the cocktail party, thinking about the Jordan couple.

"Damn that big Indian Superintendent. I'll have to watch out for him, maybe push him in front of some moving equipment. Then there was that Neanderthal at the cocktail party that threatened me just because I groped his girlfriend. How about that Patricia? She spoke French and knew Montreal, and she was a looker. It looked like she and her husband were both on the run from authorities. I'll see if I can get to know them - it might be to my advantage later."

LaBatt smiled to himself.

"I'll bet I can persuade Patricia to get something on with me. After all, who could resist?"

In January 1968, Franco BonNuit (AKA Francois LaBatt) had decided that Canada was not a safe haven so had answered an advertisement for an inspector on a project in Bolivia. His lack of truthful responses and the urgency of filling the position worked to his advantage in that he was immediately put on the payroll and shipped to Bolivia, slipping out of the net that surrounded him. His employer neglected to check his background. He talked a very good story.

Francois was feeling exuberant as he had escaped the clutches of those who had been hot on his heels. He had a new name courtesy of the Canadian justice system. He did not realize that both the Canadian and the U.S. governments were extremely interested in apprehending him. He was just hoping he could shake this contractor down for a few dollars, as he had previous ones. When this job was finished, he could disappear into the hinterlands of South America. After all, a good looking guy with a nice mustache who spoke the language and had money could do anything he wanted. The only problem was Provo.

CHAPTER 50

Early the previous Monday morning, George Jordan had walked into the hotel bar and sat down beside Francois LaBatt.

"Francois LaBatt, or is it Franco BonNuit, that I have the pleasure of meeting this morning?" questioned George.

"Who the hell are you to call me by that name?" growled LaBatt. "Do I know you from somewhere?"

"No! We've never met officially, but let me introduce myself, so that there will be no question of how I know you. I am Inspector George Jordan of the Fugitive Division of the Surete du Quebec. I am here to arrest you and take you back to Montreal."

"That is pure bull shit. You are an Argentine and have no authority to arrest me or even accuse me of anything. I'm leaving now so don't screw with me."

LaBatt started to stand up when he felt something hard against his ribs.

"Just so you don't get the idea that I am not serious. That is a gun against your ribs and I will use it if necessary," said George in a low voice.

George led LaBatt out to LaBatt's Jeep.

"You get in behind the wheel and drive. I'll be here beside you with the gun, so don't try anything."

They both got into the Jeep, with George making sure that LaBatt got behind the wheel ready to drive.

"Shit," thought LaBatt, "I will have to wait until we get to a deserted street before I can get out of this mess".

As they drove along a back street, LaBatt brought the jeep to a sudden stop. While the Jeep was still moving he reached his hand down to his left boot and retrieved a .22 caliber pistol. He took the opportunity of the sudden stop to turn to his right and fire the pistol at the back of George's head. The bullet did not kill George immediately but did leave him paralyzed.

"What was that noise, sounded like a small balloon bursting," thought George.

"It was that gun he has in his hand. Can't feel anything, must be shock. Damn it, I didn't frisk the bastard and he had a gun stuck in his boot. I should have known better. I seem to be paralyzed, can't move my arms or legs. I wonder where he plans to dump my body," thought George as he was fighting unconsciousness.

"Damn, he splattered blood all over my good jacket. He won't last long anyway. I'll get rid of him up on the cumbre. Let him drive off the side of the mountain. That will serve him right. Maybe he will be still alive when he goes over the edge and will enjoy the ride," muttered LaBatt to himself. It was doubtful that George could hear him or would be likely to reply.

LaBatt drove up the road scattering pebbles and dirt at every curve. He was a little late so he would not be catching Provo before he got to the cumbre. About a half hour later he arrived at the cumbre, after meeting a truck with bales of coca a few hundred yards from the cumbre. He looked around to make sure that no other vehicles were coming from either direction, swung the front of the Canadian Engineering Jeep over to face the edge of the road. He pulled George over to the driver's side. George was still breathing and moaned when he was moved, but could only blink his eyes. LaBatt put the transmission in low gear and let the clutch out, making sure that he was free of the Jeep. The Jeep started rolling over the edge of the road and gained speed as it dove toward the canyon 500 feet below.

George's last thoughts were of the Jeep careening over into the canyon, and the door flying off when it hit an outcropping boulder. Everything faded out as he was propelled out of the Jeep and subsequently fell down the slope below the crushed vehicle.

LaBatt watched the Jeep cartwheel down the slope. A look of complete satisfaction lit up LaBatt's face. He then walked down the road about a mile and sat down to await the next truck headed for Cochabamba. He only had to wait for about an hour for a truck to come down the road. The driver saw a dark haired gringo with a black mustache standing in the middle of the road signaling him to stop. The gringo asked if he could get a ride back to Cochabamba as his car had broken down. He was willing to pay $100.00 US to the driver if he could get a ride. For that kind of money the driver would probably take him to LaPaz if he wanted. Such extravagance, but Juan Patino was not about to refuse such a great fortune, nor was he going to ask where the broken down car was, or why his jacket was bloody.

LaBatt arrived in Cochabamba before noon. He immediately went to his apartment to change out of his blood soaked jacket.

LaBatt left his apartment, walking to the Hotel Via Tunari. He checked at the desk and asked if Patricia Jordan was in her room. The desk clerk said that she was in room #245. LaBatt went up the stairs to her room. He knocked on the door.

"Yes, who's there?" Patricia asked.

"This is Francois LaBatt. I have some very grave news for you. Please let me in and I will tell you about the accident that your husband was in."

Patricia opened the door and let him into the room.

LaBatt proceeded to tell her that her husband had been in a very serious auto accident and was asking for her.

"I don't have any transportation, so you will have to drive, OK?" LaBatt asked.

"My car is just around the corner in the hotel garage, hurry."

Patricia drove out of the garage, and then asked LaBatt for directions

Francois very smoothly directed her to the block that he lived on. He told her he had to stop at his apartment for a minute to pick up some paperwork. When she stopped the car, he got out and walked to her side of the car.

"Please get out of the car and come in with me."

When she looked at him in disbelief, he showed her his pistol and told her to get out without any noise or fuss. She was to go with him into his apartment now, or he would take her in by force. Patricia did as she was told, walking very stiffly into the house.

"Your husband told me he was a cop and tried to arrest me so I shot him and ran him over a cliff. Are you a cop too?"

Patricia said, "Yes, I am also an Inspector in the Fugitive Division of the Surete du Quebec. You are now a very wanted man. You can't escape, no matter where you go."

"I will make you sorry that you ever came to Bolivia, but first I am going to teach you what it is to have a Frenchman make love to you. You had better be good, because if you aren't, I will leave you where I did your husband. Just don't let me get tired of you too soon."

Francois tied her securely to the head board and foot board of the bed. He then went out to get groceries enough to last them a few days.

DICK ROBERTS

He assaulted her four or five times a day for the next week. He tormented her in as many ways as he could devise.

CHAPTER 51

A week later, after he had beaten her into submission, leaving her bleeding with broken ribs and torn joints, he became tired of her and, after shooting her, he left the apartment. The bullet had grazed her rib cage and left a rather ugly furlough in her side, but otherwise left her alive, seething at the thought of LaBatt. As soon as he had left the room, she found that some of the bindings were loose. She freed herself and staggered out of the building, found her car and drove off in it. She parked where she could see LaBatt when he left the building.

As he walked along the street, he realized that he had a problem in that he did not have any transportation. The rental car that the Jordans had would be too easy to locate. He noted that the Jordan's car was gone, but did not concern himself with that small detail. He needed a different car to make his getaway.

Carrie had just finished shopping for food for the next few days. Al had made a fast trip to the job site and had returned to town in the late afternoon, joined her at the market.

LaBatt saw Carrie Longstreet leaving a corner market and heading to the red Toyota Land Cruiser.

"This is the answer to all my problems, a car and a hostage. What else could I hope for?"

Al Provo came out of the corner market just in time to see Carrie being hustled into her Land Cruiser at gun point. He couldn't get to her in time. The Land Cruiser took off down the street.

A police car raced up the Prado, passing Al and heading on to answer the urgent call of a neighbor of LaBatt's. The man said that he had heard screaming in the house next door. The screams had come from Patricia Jordan. The police officer found where she had been tied up on the bed, but could not find her.

Al was told of this when a few minutes later he called the chief with the information about Carrie's abduction.

The only help that Jamie Perez could provide at that moment was that a red Toyota Land Cruiser was seen racing out of town on the old Santa Cruz highway that goes past Punata and Incallajta.

Al found Severeno and commandeered the jeep. He headed up the highway, driving as fast as he dared. He knew that he would have to stop at the police check station at Punata but hoped rather that Perez would have called ahead or he could bluff his way through. It would also be a source of information as to whether the red Toyota had passed and how long ago. The highway was paved but had no guardrails or lane markings.

Al coasted up to a stop at the police check station. He identified himself then asked the guard, "Have you seen a red Toyota Land Cruiser come past here in the past few hours? There would have been a woman driving it and a dark haired man with a black mustache riding with her."

"Jefe Perez called and said that you were on your way here. Yes, we did see the red Toyota. It passed here about a half hour ago. The woman asked if the road to Incayacta was passable. Before I could answer her, she drove off like she was in a big hurry," said the guard.

Al thanked the guard and continued on down the road. An hour later as he was approaching the turn off for Incayacta, he saw a big red hat with an embroidered hat band. He stopped to retrieve it. It was the hat that he had given Carrie in LaPaz. Al turned up the side road and saw the young boy they had given food to last week. The boy recognized him. Al asked the boy if he had seen Carrie. The boy said that she had driven up to the parking area, and she and a man with a black mustache had walked over into the ruins and were now at the large community house foundations.

Al did not notice that another Jeep was careening down the highway behind him. If he had taken the time to look, he would have seen that it was Severeno, intent on catching up with Al before Al got himself killed.

Al walked silently up to the red Toyota. Opening the door, he found that Carrie's .45 Colt was under the drivers' seat. The ignition key was still in the ignition. Al pulled the pistol out of the Toyota and stuck it under his belt. He then took the ignition key to make certain that LaBatt would not drive the Toyota away.

Al crawled up over the ridge that lay between him and the ruins. He wanted to see but not be seen. He could hear LaBatt and Carrie talking in the ruins of the community house. LaBatt was threatening Carrie, telling her that she had better do as he told her or he would kill her right there.

"Your boyfriend is very lucky, I missed him three times; otherwise he would be dead. I thought he was the cop that was after me."

Carrie told him, "You've walked into a blind alley and can't get out without me alive and well as a hostage. Al will not be very far behind us and believe me when I say that you don't really want him after you"

LaBatt lunged at Carrie only to be hit solidly just above the right temple by an oblong rock in Carrie's hand. The rock knocked LaBatt to the ground, leaving him completely disoriented for several minutes. Several minutes was all the time that Carrie needed to slip over the foundation and land on the goat trail that led down to the river bottom and the shaman's cave. Carrie made a rapid decent to the cave and hid inside before LaBatt came to his senses.

LaBatt crawled up onto his knees and staggered to his feet, trying to figure out what had happened and where Carrie had gone.

"That bitch hit me with a rock. I'll fix her ass when I find her."

He picked up his pistol and staggered around the ruined community house foundation calling her name.

"Carrie, come out here and I won't hurt you, but if I have to come and get you, you will wish you had done what I told you to. God damn it! Come out here now. I am starting to get real pissed off at you," LaBatt shouted.

He was getting very red faced now and was starting to worry that his plans might have been screwed up by Carrie.

"It's a good thing her boy friend, Provo, wasn't around. Killing him would only complicate matters."

LaBatt continued to search the many stone foundations for hiding places that could conceal Carrie, calling her name as he searched.

Al had crawled behind the ridge on the far side of the river to the place that Carrie had shown him as being the access to a goat trail down to the river. Just as he was about to crawl over the ridge and descend to the river, he heard a slight noise behind him. He swung around with his pistol pointed toward the noise. Much to his surprise, there was Severeno, packing an AK 47.

Al whispered to Severeno, "What are you doing here? I thought that I left you in Cochabamba."

Severeno said, "Chief Perez and many policemen are on their way here. They should be here in half an hour."

Al answered, "I'm going to go down to the river. I hope that Carrie got away from LaBatt and is holed up in an old cave she showed me last week. I have her pistol from the Toyota as well as the keys so LaBatt can't get away that way. If I find her, then I'll work my way back up the trail on the other side and flush LaBatt out. If you can position yourself where you can watch the ruins, you'll probably get a good shot at him."

"If you find Carrie in the cave, just stay there until the shooting is over, OK? That's what the chief wants you to do."

Al reluctantly agreed and scurried down onto the trail to the river. He was afraid that the pebbles he kept knocking off the trail into the river would alert LaBatt. He was very fortunate in that LaBatt was on the other side of the ruins and didn't hear him.

The river just below the falls was rather wide and very shallow. He was able to wade across and get to the trail on the far side. He sidled along the narrow trail, nearly falling off several times. He found the cave that Carrie had shown him. He called softly to Carrie. She answered after he had called her name for the third time. He crawled into the small opening to find his feet on a relatively flat floor and able to stand up. Carrie came up out of the darkness to wrap her arms around him and to hug him in happiness that he had found her and that she did not have to worry about LaBatt any more. All she wanted was for Al to engulf her in his arms and to kiss her and to love her forever. She hoped that she would be able to repay him for saving her. She was certainly going to try.

Unknown to Al, LaBatt and the police, Patricia had followed the parade of police cars to Incayacta. She parked down the hill well hidden from the retinue and climbed to a high point where she could see everything that was going on. She had removed a scoped hunting rifle from the back of her car. It was a caliber .270, a flat shooting bullet that was good out to about 1,000 yards. She found a likely boulder about 600 yards from LaBatt. She laid the rifle on her folded up coat on the top of the boulder, and waited. Her chance came as LaBatt started down the trail toward Al.

Patricia gently squeezed the trigger and the rifle barked sharply at the exact time that Al and the police were firing at LaBatt. She knew that she had not missed. If they examined the body closely, they would find a small hole passing completely through his chest. She now had extracted her revenge for her brother's death and would be able to enjoy the $1,000,000 that the Canadian Mafia had paid to be rid of LaBatt. Patricia walked back to her rented car, put the rifle in the trunk and drove off down the road to a new future in Argentina.

Al and Carrie suddenly heard gunfire from above in the ruins. Chief Perez had apparently arrived with the cavalry. Al stuck his head out of the cave opening and saw LaBatt struggling down the trail with his left arm hanging limp and blood running from a wound in his side. He still grasped his pistol, and when he saw Al, LaBatt swung the pistol around in his right hand. Al did not hesitate. He fired his .45 Colt, hitting LaBatt squarely in the chest. LaBatt fell off the trail into the river, floating a few feet until he beached on a sand bar.

Perez and group came charging down the trail, waving their guns menacingly. Al called out very loudly that he was on their side and for them not to shoot. Chief Perez rounded the corner just in time to stop any further gunfire. They helped Al and Carrie up the trail and to their cars. They then fished LaBatt's body out of the river. Severeno stood nearby with a very self-satisfied grin on his face.

Carrie held onto Al as if her life depended on his being next to her. She definitely was not going to let him out of her sight, even for a minute. They went to Carrie's Toyota and Carrie asked Al to drive as she did not feel up to it. Al replaced her .45 Colt under the front seat, drew the keys out of his pocket, and helped her into the jeep.

He turned to Chief Perez. "Will you see to having Severeno return the BOSCO jeep to town? I'll drive Senorita Longstreet back to her home. I may be busy for awhile. I'll drop by your office tomorrow to file a complete report if you need one."

Chief Perez smiled and replied, "Severeno will provide the report. No need to involve you in this mess. By the way, Senorita Jordan will be just fine. She will be going back to Montreal next week." How little did he know.

As Al was walking back to Carrie's Toyota, he looked toward the mountains and glimpsed a giant Andean Condor gliding aloft on the ever present thermals, still looking for a meal. Another omen.

CHAPTER 52

"Thank God that you came through that ordeal uninjured. You had me very worried for a while," said Al.

Carrie reached over to kiss him and said, "I wasn't afraid because I knew that you would be there for me. My only worry was that you would do something heroic and get yourself killed. That I could not accept."

Carrie made a late breakfast the next morning for the two of them after they had returned to the safety of her home.

During breakfast Al told her, "I have to go to the job for a while to work some things out with Bob. When I return, we can go up Mt. Tunari for a picnic. How would you like that - a chance to be alone away from all the troubles of the world?"

"I would like that very much, just to be away from prying maids, considerate neighbors, and nosy newspaper reporters. Just us."

Al drove up to the job and was met by Bob asking him what had been going on. Bob said he and Agnes had been worried about Al and Carrie after they heard that Carrie had been made a hostage by LaBatt.

It took Al about a half hour to explain all the happenings of the day before. He told Bob about seeing Carrie being pushed into her Toyota by LaBatt at gun point and Al's pursuit of the two of them to Incayacta. He told of Severeno showing up and then Chief Perez with the police force and the rather abrupt demise of LaBatt.

Bob told Al, "The TBM is now advancing daily at 90 to 100 feet through very good rock. That should please the leaders in San Francisco. Will you be staying around for a while? I almost forgot. I have another message for you from Major Wolf. He wants you to call him ASAP. What is that all about?" Bob asked. "Does that mean that you will be leaving soon?"

"I have no idea what my leader in San Francisco or the good Major want. I will just play it by ear. If they want me to do something that interferes with my life and that of Carrie, I will probably tell them all to take a flying leap."

Al called Major Wolf from the office and was told that the Major wanted to meet him at the hotel bar on the Prado at 1:30 PM.

"I am going on a sabbatical. See you when I get back in a few years."

Al drove back to Carrie's home, very glad to walk in the front door to her open arms.

"Bob and Agnes want us to go by for dinner, OK?"

The dinner ended about eleven, and Al and Carrie returned to Carrie's home.

Al held Carrie close throughout the night, trying to calm her down. Carrie was near an emotional breakdown. She had met the man of her dreams and was very afraid that she would lose him for one reason or another. By morning she had convinced herself that he would be back to her.

Carrie was having conflicting thoughts about Al. She had to admit that she loved him and should be ready to take on the future with him, regardless of the consequences. She forgot all her forebodings the moment he walked through the front door. She would be very happy to look forward to him coming through the door for the rest of her life.

THE END

EPILOGUE

He had never felt this way about anyone since his wife had died. He could see Carrie's face and her wonderful smile. He had to ask himself if he were playing fair with Carrie. She had no idea about what he did other than that he was a construction trouble shooter for a large construction company. She only knew that little about his past that was safe for her to know. She had no way of knowing whether he would survive this or any future assignments, let alone where and when he would be sent instantly to some far corner of the globe.

"I should put her behind me, and give her a chance to forget me. I can't do that so I will just say to hell with it and tell the company to piss off."

Al looked out past mountain peaks and saw a giant Andean Condor gliding along with just its wing tip feathers and its head moving.

"God, he thought, I hope I'm not like that Condor, just gliding along on the wind currents, killing to survive. And, like him never stop moving long enough to make and keep lasting relations."

That foolishness all ends here and now. I am staying with the woman I love.

ABOUT THE AUTHOR

Dick Roberts is at home anywhere in the world. During the Korean War, he served with the U. S. Army Infantry. After the war, he began his civil engineering career which took him around the world, as he built tunnels, dams, and bridges in Australia - where he and his family lived for two years, then to Bolivia - where he took his family again for two years, California, Idaho, Metro Washington, DC, and finally Atlanta. Never one to sit still, he consulted with firms in, Oregon, Boston, Washington, Singapore, New Guinea, Hong Kong, Thailand, most of Europe, and Turkey.

Dick Roberts was a Principal Professional Associate and Vice President for a major design company, with more than forty-three years of experience in heavy civil construction and design. Twenty-five of these years were spent working for contractors providing estimates and as construction project manager on major tunnels, dams, bridges, marine and hydro-electric projects worldwide. He held jobs ranging from Chief Estimator to Regional Operations Manager. Dick spent eighteen years working for design firms, providing cost estimates, schedules, and constructability reviews for mass transit tunnels, waste water tunnels, ocean outfalls, underground structures, and major bridges and highway projects.

Dick and his wife Roberta have traveled most of the known world over the past eight years, seeing those sights that he had never taken time for before retirement.